Beyond
the Night

EDEN was young and innocent as her name. The only home she knew was the tropical jungle where she helped her dedicated doctor father in his work. When he told her, suddenly, that they were to take a holiday on the enchanting island of Caravel, she was excited, overjoyed and perhaps a little apprehensive!

Caravel was all she had pictured: on the surface it was beautiful, sunny and serene. But Eden felt, uneasily, that beneath the glittering surface, ran dark currents of distrust and fear, intrigue and mystery. Somehow Justin was involved —that strange, unpredictable, charming man who was coming to mean so much to her, and in a night of tropical storm and wild terror Eden discovered the secret of Caravel—and the secret of her heart.

By the same author

THE SHINING HIGHWAY
TILL THE STARS ARE OLD

MARGARET LIVINGSTONE

Beyond the Night

The Valentine Romance Club

THE VALENTINE ROMANCE CLUB
178-202 Great Portland Street, London, W.1

*This book has been set in Baskerville type
face. It has been printed in Great Britain on
Antique Wove paper by Taylor Garnett
Evans & Co. Ltd, Watford, Herts, and
bound by them*

ONE

THE horn of a Land Rover blared impatiently while Eden Ashby was trying to finish packing in the sticky heat of a South American mission bungalow. Jungle parrots screeched a derisive answer to the summons of the horn as with a sigh of relief Eden snapped the catch of her one suitcase and hurried over to the dressing-table.

'Cheque-book, pen, wallet, compact,' she muttered, stuffing the articles into her handbag, and then she took time to glance at her reflection in the mirror and to make a face at the sight of her old silk dress. Its former white-ness had mellowed to pale cream after many washings and strong sunshine, and its only advantage was that it never dated because of the simple style. Forgetting the pacing figure of her father in the mission compound, Eden half-closed her eyes and tried to imagine how she would look in green or blue or perhaps in yellow. It was hard to believe that at nineteen years of age she possessed little but riding breeches, shirts, and a few plain dresses in white cotton or silk.

A knock at the door was followed by the entry of a middle-aged woman, stockily built and wearing a fawn linen suit.

'Aren't you ready yet?' she asked. 'Your father's opinion of women is getting lower by the minute, and here you stand admiring yourself as if tomorrow would do!'

Eden sighed softly. 'Admiring isn't exactly the word,

Nell. I know from magazines that golden hair and dark-brown eyes are what they call "interesting", but any colouring can be dull if you don't dress up to it. I hope I'll have time to do some shopping in Araquilla before the island steamer sails – I'm just beginning to realize how tired I am of tropical white and I'll probably end up gorgeously arrayed like the Queen of Sheba!'

'And give your father a heart attack? For heaven's sake don't let's start this holiday with explosions from Charles! He likes you to dress simply and you know how difficult he can be when he's crossed. Now do get a move on before he does for that car horn!'

'It's a wonder I'm ready now,' Eden said as she picked up her suitcase. 'All Father had to do was hand over a small mission hospital to another doctor for two months, but I had to explain every single dispensary and house-hold detail to his wife who's a New Yorker and terrified of the jungle! You know, I can't believe we're really leaving Guiana for a few weeks – you must have worked terribly hard on Father to get him to agree.'

'I appealed to his sense of propriety,' Nell said with a grin, 'and I told him that although I was old enough to be David's mother it wasn't quite the thing for me to share a house with him on a tropical island! Fortunately, Charles doesn't know about the times David and I have had to share a tent because we'd got separated from the rest of the expedition or because one tent blew away or sprang a leak! But seriously, I said that if he didn't let you off the chain you'd go exploring the big wide world for yourself before long.'

'Like you and David,' Eden said wistfully, leading the way out to the compound. 'Archaeology must be such fun. The two of you are just back from Peru after digging up lots of wonderful finds, and you wouldn't dream of tak-

6

ing this holiday if the rest of your party could start the Mexican expedition in under two months.'

'Maybe you'll be joining us some day,' Nell murmured, and the significance of her tone wasn't lost on Eden who flushed slightly as David Meredith hurried from the car to take her suitcase. His grey eyes held eager welcome and he placed a protective hand under her elbow as they walked to the car.

Dr Charles Ashby surveyed his daughter impatiently, and Eden half-smiled at him hoping that he wouldn't work up to one of his black moods when, according to him, the world and everything in it was out of joint, and women were the chief offenders.

'Couldn't you make up your mind what to wear on this historic journey?' he asked testily. 'Let's get started before I change my mind about the whole project. Holidays are for the weary and the unfit and as far as I'm concerned they're just a waste of time!'

Nobody said anything and he got into the front seat beside David, who was driving, while Nell and Eden sat at the back. Luggage made space rather cramped but Eden relaxed in her seat as they drove away and she lifted her face gratefully to the breeze which ruffled her short feathery curls. She wasn't unfit but she was definitely weary, and she knew that her father needed this break from routine as much as she did even if he wouldn't admit it. Occasionally they went to Araquilla on the coast for a week but never in her nineteen years had Eden been anywhere else, and seven days at a time was the longest break she had ever had from the medical mission where she had been born. Nell Macgregor, a lifelong friend of the doctor's, stayed at the mission whenever she had the chance between expeditions, and her visits had been lively colourful events along the years. She usually brought a friend or two with her, but on the past three occasions she had brought only David Meredith, now twenty-seven and making a reputation for himself in the field of archaeology.

Eden looked at the back of David's head as he sat at the wheel in front of her and her brown eyes were thoughtful. He said he was in love with her, Nell was pleased because she had wanted to bring about that very thing, and Dr Ashby approved of the courtship with a few reservations. He didn't want to lose his daughter who assisted him so capably in the hospital dispensary and who made what he called a tolerable job of housekeeping in the backwoods, but he foresaw that some day she might be left alone and he would rather know that someone like David would be taking care of her.

As for her own feelings, Eden wondered helplessly what yardstick you could use when you met so few men and when 'love' was as unreasonable and inexplicable as books and magazines said it was. Could this be 'love', this warmth she felt for David? She liked his looks, she was interested in his work, but nothing about him made her pulse beat faster and just where did fondness end and love begin or wasn't there any difference anyway?

She sat staring unseeingly ahead until she realized that they were out of the jungle and that her father's gaze was turning unwillingly but with a terrible fascination towards the view on the left of the road. There was no fence, just a sheer drop to the floor of a valley where a river glinted far below, the sides of the drop covered with boulders and scrub and a few sentinel trees. Here, thirteen years before, Mrs Charles Ashby had crashed to her death in an open touring car, and the six-year-old Eden had been flung to miraculous safety in the branches of a tree.

This was the only road to the coast and Eden believed that her father left the mission so seldom because it still

8

took all his fortitude to pass the scene of the accident which had killed his wife.

'She was my mother as well as his wife,' Eden thought, and her eyes filled with tears as David accelerated and the rigidity slowly passed from her father's shoulders and he looked though the windscreen again with a dark, sombre gaze.

'I wish we didn't have to come this way,' Nell murmured. 'But after all, it's thirteen years since it happened and it's time he stopped brooding about it.'

'Time I stopped brooding too?' Eden asked over the lump in her throat. 'It isn't possible. That dreadful day changed everything and it changed my father almost beyond recognition. He'll hardly trust me out of his sight, and if it were for love I could understand it but it's sheer possessiveness and suspicion.'

Nell sighed and touched Eden's hand. 'My dear, you must remember that he feels he has reason for it. He adored your mother, simply worshipped the ground she walked on, and then he got that note from her to say she was leaving him for her old world of the theatre and taking you with her. I honestly think that was a more searing shock to him than the news of her death on the same day. I was fond of them both and I came as soon as I could, and I give you my word I thought he would go out of his mind with anguish. You'd been returned to him almost from the dead, and it's not surprising that he has guarded you closely all your life.'

'Tell me, Nell, do you agree with Father and David that I'm a helpless innocent and that I've got to be protected from the sinful world on this holiday?'

'You must admit you haven't seen much of what you call the sinful world,' Nell said with a chuckle. 'I'm sorry you had all your education at the mission school, but your father wouldn't think of sending you away to college and

I couldn't interfere. Charles and David are only considering your welfare when they want to look after you, and you *have* led a very sheltered life.'

Eden turned a wide considering gaze on her companion.

'Can you think of anything less sheltered than working in a medical mission in the depths of the jungle, Nell? Lots of the natives aren't far removed from savagery even if they wear the trappings of civilization. Father looks on most of his patients as interesting cases although he's kind to them in a sort of distant way, and I don't suppose he's ever stopped to wonder whether I feel the same. Well, I don't. I see them all as human beings first and patients afterwards, and I've crammed a lifetime's experience of human nature into the last few years. I've seen life and birth and death, the seven deadly sins, and all the virtues there are. Do you think David has seen as much?'

'I—' Nell began and then hesitated. 'Well, I can't say I ever thought of life on a mission as being like that. But David has seen a lot of the world—'

'And I've seen life, which isn't quite the same thing. All right, Nell, I know you're on Father's side most of the time, but please don't hover over me while I'm out in the big wide world. Two guardian angels is more than enough for any girl!'

Nell smiled at her rather uncertainly and Eden wondered if she had been too forthright. But oh how tired she was of the guardian atmosphere in which she had lived for so long and which she seemed unable to escape even on holiday. The mere fact of there being a holiday at all was hard to take in, and it didn't help that the Caribbean island of Caravel sounded remote and not quite true.

David was the only one of the party who had been there before and it was through his efforts that they had been able to rent a house on the Dayspring estate. Justin Fontaine, the owner of Dayspring, was a scientist friend of one of David's colleagues, and members of the archaeological society had often spent leaves on the island. David had always been enthusiastic about Caravel and about the house which was called Wayfarers, but it seemed to Eden that there was a distinct reserve in his manner when Justin Fontaine himself was discussed. It made her curious, if only to know what could bring that look of fastidious disapproval to David's boyish pleasant features.

By the time the Land Rover topped the rise leading down to the seaport of Araquilla, Dr Ashby had recovered from his preoccupation and was ready to do battle with the authorities over the absence of the island steamer from her usual Monday berth in the harbour. Small craft skimmed busily across the sparkling water and a graceful white yacht was anchored out in the bay, but there was no sign of the squat-funnelled *Doria* which should have been almost ready to sail for the islands smudged on the far horizon.

Nell and Eden strolled on the pier while the men went to call on the shipping agent, but David soon came out to say that schedules had been altered and the island steamer called at Araquilla on Fridays instead of Mondays.

David grinned at Eden. 'I'm afraid your father's a bit mad about it, but as the agent said, if we'd bothered to inquire earlier we'd have been told of the new sailings.'

'Oh well, there are worse hotels than the Harbour House,' Eden said philosophically, 'and at least we'll have time to do some shopping here. What about Mr Fontaine? Had you told him when to expect us?'

'I didn't mention a day,' David told her, 'but as I said we'd be arriving this week I reckon he won't expect us until the steamer gets to Caravel next Friday. Pity there isn't any other way of getting to the island but it's too small to have an airfield and I don't suppose it would pay any charter company to run an air service there anyway.'

When Dr Ashby came out of the shipping office he agreed rather gloomily that there was nothing else to do but stay at the hotel until Friday, and as they turned to leave the pier Nell looked out at the white yacht once more.

'Anyone know who owns it?' she asked. 'Imagine possessing anything so gorgeous!'

'It belongs to a chap called Clyde Dinsmore,' Dr Ashby said. 'He's an American with business interests all over this continent and the agent just told me he's inspecting one of his coffee plantations in the interior at the moment. He spent a few days at the mission once when he had a bout of malaria – interesting type of man, not so keen on money as on power but the way things work out for him he gets both. I wonder if he'll be calling at the islands?'

'I hope not,' Eden said, wrinkling her nose. 'I couldn't stand him and he'd be the perfect serpent in any paradise.'

'A very rash judgement, my child,' her father said drily. 'There's more to that man than anyone with your inexperience could fathom.'

They were entering the foyer of the hotel and Eden said no more about Clyde Dinsmore. She hadn't needed experience of men to know that he was hard and ruthless and that his *bonhomie* was no more than a mask under which he studied with a cold calculation how he might use his fellow-man to the best advantage.

After they had inspected their rooms and freshened up after the journey, Eden and Nell went first to the bank and then to see what Araquilla could offer in the way of clothes. Nell had a good collection of immaculate linen suits and she seldom wore anything else, but she had a weakness for barbaric jewellery and was always on the look-out for a piece which would go with her no-nonsense and rather weather-beaten appearance.

'You've got an odd sort of gleam in your eye,' Nell said as she followed Eden down a street leading off the main plaza. 'Just what have you in mind?'

'Clothes,' Eden said blithely, 'and I know where to find the materials I want. I've mooned over them when I've stayed here before but I decided they weren't worth the unholy row Father would make. But I was younger then, and it will be interesting to see how far he'll go in insisting that I wear what *he* likes regardless of what I feel about it.'

'Interesting!' Nell groaned. 'What's come over you? You've got all your life in front of you, and why must you stir the poor man into saying more than he means to say? He's had more than his share of trouble already. '

About to retort that Nell would follow where Charles Ashby led, Eden held her peace. It wouldn't be fair to tease Nell about something she thought so well concealed.

'It hasn't been all milk and honey for me either,' she said briefly, and led the way into Kharama's 'Indian Bazaar'.

Nell gravitated to the trays of bracelets and brooches at the rear of the shop, and Eden hesitated as she looked up at the tall Indian who had come forward.

'I want something beautiful,' she said after a moment, her voice breathless and eager. 'I've seen your materials before, but now I want to buy some. I can't look at them all so would you suggest some for me to choose from?'

Kharama bowed, smiling his satisfaction as he glanced from Eden to the bales of material everywhere. Her colouring of pale gold hair, brown eyes, and honey-tanned skin was unusual in Araquilla and it gratified Kharama's artistic soul to produce the best he had.

'For a sari?' he suggested as she gazed spellbound at a shimmering piece of golden gauze. 'For a special occasion of course. And I have ear-rings which are the exact shade of this green border.'

'But – I couldn't wear a sari!'

'Why not? Are tartans to be left to the Scots, fur hats to the Russians, mandarin coats to the Chinese? Come, I will show you.'

Skilfully he draped the gold tissue around her and when he had finished she stared wide-eyed at the reflection in the long mirror to which he led her. Nell came across and peered over her shoulder.

'Why, Eden, you look like a stranger,' she said, and her voice was oddly uncertain as if for the first time ever she had lost sight of the little unsophisticated girl she had always known.

'Magnificent,' Kharama murmured, unwinding the golden folds. 'You could of course make it into an ortho-dox Western dress but it would seem a pity to touch it with scissors. We should make use of beauty from wher-ever it comes. Now, I have also a gown of Chinese bro-cade in the blue of the larkspur threaded with silver. It is wide of sleeve, and a gown of great dignity and beauty. I do not show these garments to the ordinary tourist. I keep them for occasions such as this.'

Nell raised her eyebrows in cynical disbelief but Eden smiled happily. She knew that Kharama would make a very nice profit out of all she bought, but she also knew that his words were sincere and that he was enjoying this as much as she was. She bought the gold tissue, the Chinese gown, and several dress lengths of other materials while Nell rummaged among the displays of jewellery.

Kharama went to make up the parcel and Eden turned to see her companion trying on a barbaric silver necklace.

'That one's too heavy, Nell,' she said. 'Have the blue stone pendant if you must have one at all. You dig up such fabulous relics for museums all over the country but you can never resist a pedlar's tray!'

Nell made a face at her own reflection in a shell-ornamented mirror. 'I love pretty things but they don't go with my features or my age. As for my archaeological finds, my conscience wouldn't let me keep a piece of jewellery which had once belonged to an Inca priestess!'

Eden laughed and touched the gold medallion which hung on a fine chain round her neck.

'Nell, thou shalt not covet! Anyway, this necklace is unique and we don't know for sure that it is an Inca piece. You must admit that it looks better on me than in a glass case in some fusty museum!'

The older woman merely grunted and as she turned away to examine a display of bracelets Eden dropped to a stool and sat fingering the medallion, her thoughts far away.

Old Dyqui, the Indian who had given her the gold piece, had been odd-job man at the mission for years. He had arrived there as a guide, liked the place and the people, and stayed on. Round his neck he always wore a small leather pouch containing, so he said, his charm to ward off evil. Nobody ever saw the charm until he lay dying in his little hut in the mission compound, and then the only person he wanted near him was Eden. From the day of her birth he had adored and served the small golden-haired girl, and now he wanted her to have the only treasure he possessed.

'I have no family,' he told her in the dialect which was as natural to her as English, 'and it is not fitting that this beauty should go into the darkness with me. When my spirit has flown you will take the little bag and when you look at that which is inside it you will remember Dyqui. Your hair is the colour of the sun – perhaps you also are descended from the Virgins of the Sun God – even as Dyqui is of the family of the great Atahualpa himself.'

When the old man was gone, Dr Ashby brought the small pouch to the dispensary and handed it to his daughter.

'Would you like me to open it?' he asked. 'You know what Indians are like when it comes to charms. This could be just a few feathers, perhaps a small bone or two, or some dried-up roots.'

'Even so,' Eden said with a little smile, 'it was his only possession and he left it to me with his love. Did you know that he believed he was descended from the royal line of the Inca?'

'Oh, beliefs!' her father said tolerantly. 'Indians never know when their legends becomes facts in their own minds—'

He stared as Eden held the pouch upside-down and a medallion slid on to the table to lie glittering and golden in the sunlight. It was about the size of a crown piece, smoothly circular in the centre and edged with delicate points to represent the rays of the sun.

'My dear girl!' Dr Ashby exclaimed. 'I'm no authority on the subject but I'd swear this is centuries old! Apart from its face value it must be priceless as an antique.'

'Oh I never want to know how much it's worth in money! I shall wear it always like Dyqui did, only I shall have it on a gold chain. Most of the time it won't be seen because I shall wear it underneath my dress, but on high days and holidays – if we ever have any! – I'll wear it as a necklace.'

'All right, if that's what you want to do with it I'll give

you a gold chain for your next birthday. Although Dyqui didn't wear it, somebody did – once. It's as smooth as glass on the back and there are two little openings for a cord or chain to go through.'

So Eden got her gold chain and it was then that she discovered that the smooth back of the medallion could be separated from the ornamented front. The rim which kept the two sides together was indiscernible, the same beautiful craftsmanship which marked the enduring massive granite walls of the ancient lost cities of South America. But Eden told no one of the small cavity she had found. It was just a pleasant secret to share with a dream-distant Daughter of the Sun God.

She came out of her reverie to see Kharama beside her with her parcel.

'It would give me great pleasure to deliver this later in the evening,' he said, and she smiled at him.

'That's very kind of you, but I'd like to take it back with me now and gloat over it! I'll probably call again – we'll be here until the Caravel steamer leaves on Friday.'

'And the time goes slowly in Araquilla! My brother lives on Caravel and I go to see him when I can get away from business. Even on a dark night my small boat can do the crossing in five hours—'

He stopped abruptly as if he had said more than he meant to, and Eden grinned at him. He and his brother probably ran a very profitable smuggling exchange between the island and the mainland 'on a dark night'.

'Safe journey next time you go,' she said in a stage whisper and his dark eyes twinkled as Nell came over and joined them.

'Let's get back to the hotel,' Eden said to her. 'We'll find you a gorgeous piece of glass jewellery before we leave here!'

She was eager to get her parcel into the safety of her

room before her father asked any awkward questions, and she groaned inwardly when she saw him sitting in the lounge with Clyde Dinsmore and David.

'He doesn't look all that bad,' Nell murmured when Eden told her this was the owner of the yacht she had admired, and she smiled graciously as Dinsmore rose and bowed with old-world gallantry.

'Good news, Eden,' Dr Ashby said with satisfaction. 'Mr Dinsmore is leaving for Caravel with the yacht tomorrow and he has offered to take us with him.'

'But will the house be ready?' Eden asked. 'Mr Fontaine isn't expecting us until Friday.'

'Oh, he won't mind us being early,' David told her. 'We may have to do without household staff for a day or two but that won't kill any of us!'

'It's very kind of you to take us, Mr Dinsmore,' Eden said, knowing that she couldn't hold out against the eager acceptance of the idea by the others.

'It is a great pleasure to me, Miss Ashby,' he said, his curiously opaque eyes regarding her with no expression at all. Apart from his size there was an oppressive power about this man, and Eden found her old instinctive dislike returning in full force. It was a relief when he turned to David and she was free of his heavy-lidded scrutiny.

'Mr Meredith, did I hear you mention Justin Fontaine? He has quite a reputation as a scientist in the States – seems odd that he should bury himself on a small island like Caravel when he could be a leading light in the scientific world back home.'

'Oh well, Caravel is his home and he has a lovely old house called Dayspring,' David said. 'He doesn't have to work for the cash and I was told that he had some sort of conscientious objections to the government projects he had to take on in Florida – I never knew if it was missiles or gas or what it was. Anyway, he packed it in and set up his own lab on Caravel where he does independent research on agricultural preparations.'

'Yes,' Dinsmore said thoughtfully. 'Some of his work in that line has been quite revolutionary. One of my companies was interested in a fruit-spray he developed but when they went after it Fontaine had already sold it to the government for practically nothing. It sure is refreshing to come across a man of science who works just for the fun of it.'

David nodded. 'He's got some odd ideas about what he calls the ethics of warfare and that's why he won't do any work on atoms and hydrogen and all that stuff. We'd still be at the bow-and-arrow stage if he had his way!'

Eden sat back and listened as the discussion went from agriculture to space-rockets and back to Justin Fontaine and she noticed that Dinsmore was doing far more listening than talking.

'I only know Fontaine by reputation,' he said at one point, 'but it seems that his personal reputation isn't so good! The last time I was on Caravel the place was buzzing with a story about him and some coloured girl.'

Dr Ashby looked at David with a frown, and David's fair skin flushed as he cast an apologetic glance at Eden.

'I've heard that rumour,' he admitted, 'but it was none of my business—'

'I think it may be my business,' Dr Ashby said stiffly. 'I left all the arrangements for this vacation to you and it is rather disturbing to find that we are renting a house which is next door to that of a man with a loose character. I think you had better tell me all you know about him before we go any farther.'

Eden knew that it was on her account that her father was upset and she looked balefully at Dinsmore who was as calm as ever and who seemed to be watching the situation with interest. It would be quite unbearable if the whole idea of a holiday on Caravel fell through because of something which was no one's concern but that of the man involved in unsavoury rumours. David ran nervous fingers through his brown hair, said he didn't know Justin intimately, and then as Dr Ashby just sat waiting he went on to tell what he knew.

Justin Fontaine was thirty-six and unmarried. His mother had been English and his father of French stock from New Orleans, and both of them died within a few years of each other because there was no hospital on Caravel and they had been taken to Trinidad too late for expert medical attention to save them. So Justin had built and endowed a small hospital on the island, and among the applications for posts had come two from Brazil. They were from two Austrian doctors who had fled from Nazi Europe years before and had found refuge in South America. Having taken up their references and qualifications, Justin was delighted to bring them to the security of Caravel, and while Dr Zeitler lived at the hospital, Dr Brandt lived with Justin at Dayspring where his daughter Kara kept house for them both.

'It's a very respectable household,' David said rather desperately. 'I mean, apart from these rumours Mr Dinsmore mentioned there's nothing to indicate that Justin — that Fontaine isn't a — well, a perfect gentleman. We'll hardly see anything of him anyway because he really does work hard in that lab of his, and he only used to drop in at Wayfarers last time I was there because one of my colleagues was an old friend of his.'

'I see,' Dr Ashby murmured. 'Well, maybe there's no reason why we should have much to do with him. I'm the last man to condemn anyone on hearsay so we'll just leave matters as they are for the time being.'

'Splendid!' Dinsmore exclaimed. 'I wouldn't have said anything only I thought the story was well known. I'll be staying for a short vacation with my friend Paul Randolph on Caravel so I sure hope I can meet this Fontaine.'

Long cool drinks were served and soon afterwards Dinsmore left for his yacht, the *Rosca*. He hoped they didn't mind leaving early in the morning and he would have a launch to meet them at the wharf at six o'clock.

Nell's enthusiasm had waned somewhat by the time Dinsmore took his leave.

'Not my type after all,' she said. 'I got the feeling that he wasn't the man to confer a favour for nothing, but what is there about us that could interest him?'

'David's knowledge of Justin Fontaine,' replied Eden. 'He very cleverly brought the conversation back to him every time it strayed to something else.'

'Imagination!' David scoffed. 'Dinsmore is a big noise in the manufacture of agricultural chemicals and it's only natural he'd be interested in Fontaine's work. I can't say I like Dinsmore but to me he's just a typical business tycoon with an eye on the main chance.'

Eden didn't argue, almost afraid to say much in case her father decided against Caravel after all. She retrieved her parcel from where she had left it at the reception desk after her father had gone upstairs and she managed to get all her new fabrics into her half-empty suitcase. They spent the rest of the day quietly and when night came Eden lay in bed listening to the swish of small waves on the beach and wondering how much of her life would have changed before she returned to the mission deep in the jungle of Guiana. Her father had two months' leave and by the end of it she should know how much – or how little – David Meredith mattered in her world. Not that either David or Nell would be able to relax completely. They would be compiling a report for the geographical society which had financed their last expedition and they meant to make a start on the book they had been planning for some time. But Wayfarers which was on the boundary of the Dayspring estate was big enough to keep them all from falling over each other, and small enough to preserve an intimate atmosphere.

With a sigh of anticipation Eden closed her eyes, aware that at least the following weeks would hold experiences very different from those she had known in Guiana.

They left the hotel when the swift tropical dawn lightened the sky and they saw the launch coming in to the wharf. Two smart members of the crew stowed the baggage aboard, and when they reached the yacht Dinsmore was waiting for them at the top of the accommodation ladder. The trip was pleasant enough with Dinsmore exerting himself to be a good host and entertaining companion, and when the *Rosca* sailed along the coastline of Caravel he came to stand beside Eden at the rail, pointing out places of interest. Although he hadn't met many local inhabitants when he had stayed there before he had seen quite a bit of the place itself. The only port was at Kinghorn and from there they would have to travel by road to the Dayspring estate which was on the far side of the island.

'It's only about eight miles,' Dinsmore said. 'And as it can't be any more than twenty miles the other way I reckon you won't get lost on Caravel! I'm sorry I can't take you all the way but Kinghorn is the only spot where a yacht this size can put in.'

'Oh but it's lovely to get here so much sooner than we expected. Anyway, David says there's a good taxi service so it shouldn't take long to reach Dayspring. I do like what I've seen of the island – all those sandy beaches round the point, and the way the houses are built up the hillsides. It makes me think of the old hymn, "where every prospect pleases"!'

' "And only man is vile"?' David quoted wickedly as he came to stand on her other side. 'I trust that you except present company?'

'Naturally,' Eden murmured. 'Well, I'm a bit wind-blown, so if you'll excuse me I'll go and freshen up before we land.'

She went below to the lavish powder-room, wishing that David hadn't made it quite so obvious that 'present company' had been under discussion probably to its detriment. Dinsmore had glanced at them sharply as if seeking to understand the significance in David's mischievous tones, and for no reason that she could think of Eden didn't want Dinsmore to know how she felt about him.

She shrugged as she sat down in front of the mirror and ran a comb through her short feathery curls. Probably she needed a holiday and that was why her imagination was working overtime. She applied fresh lipstick, straightened the belt of her old silk dress, and then turned to smile at Nell who had just come in.

'You'll do,' Nell grunted. 'You know, I've just been shown over this floating palace and I'm beginning to wonder if I've gone after the wrong things in life. You accused me yesterday of breaking the tenth commandment but it's shattered in very small pieces right now! I covet my neighbour's yacht and his manservants and his maidservants and his ox and his ass – if he's got any! – and I wouldn't give you sixpence for the biggest archaeological find of the century.'

'Oh yes you would! One just has to mention the name "Peru" and your eyes light up as they never did for any old boat. Come on, we're nearly at the pier and I want to make a pretty speech to our host. He deserves it after all, because Araquilla would have become rather deadly by the time the steamer turned up.'

The pierhead and the road beyond seemed to be one bustle of life and colour, and judging by the row of ramshackle cars which had just raced into position there would be no difficulty in finding transport to Dayspring.

They hired a car big enough to take all four of them plus the baggage, and with a final wave to Clyde Dinsmore who stood on the deck of the *Rosca* they set off along the rather rough road which wound upwards once it left Kinghorn behind. The mountain was steep but the road twisted and turned through dense scrub until they came to a pass near the top of the range where they could see the far side of the island spread out before them like a relief map. Here were the cocoa plantations with their shading of tall immortelle trees which were now a mass of scarlet blossom; the lime and the coconut plantations which showed a glimpse of white colonial-style houses through the foliage; and beyond the valleys and gentle hillsides the sea sparkled in the morning sunshine and fell in a line of creaming surf on the bays curved round the coast.

'How lovely,' Eden said with a sigh of satisfaction. 'The harbour at Kinghorn doesn't prepare one for this.'

'That was merely Kinghorn County,' David told her. 'You are now in Amberley County and that of course is where all the best people live! Dayspring is over there to the west, and that long white building on the headland is the hospital. Our little house is on a point of land jutting out to sea, so we have water on three sides although the gardens all round are quite extensive.'

Wayfarers was a two-storeyed house with a pillared veranda on the upper floor which formed the roof of the terrace on the ground floor. It was all white with window-shutters of pale blue, and against this quiet background flowering shrubs and vines glowed scarlet and blue and yellow. The surf swished gently on the sandy beach below the house, and the breeze swayed palm fronds on their long slender stems.

'I'll go and see about keys,' David said as the car drove off. 'Someone at the big house is bound to know about us even if I can't find our landlord. He'll probably be in his lab at this hour and I know from experience that he doesn't encourage visitors!'

There were several paths leading up through trees or bushes from the little promontory, and after David had gone out of sight the others strolled through the picturesque wild gardens. Dr Ashby and Nell retired to the shade of the terrace after a few minutes and Eden made for a bluff where she thought she might get a good view of the surrounding countryside. It was a gentle climb and at the top she stood among the scattered slender palms, enjoying the tranquillity of the morning. She walked slowly in the direction from which she thought David would come, identifying the wild flowers which grew in such profusion on either side of the path, and halting sometimes beside unfamiliar blooms.

It was while she was stooping down to have a closer look at the carpet of blue almost like English hyacinths that she saw the wet splotch of crimson on a pale green leaf. It must have landed there very recently to look so fresh and with a shiver of apprehension Eden stood up and glanced about her.

An injury to a small animal? Or to a person? A few paces beyond the hyacinths, leaves and grass had a bruised appearance as if someone or something had passed heavily by. The only sounds were the singing of innumerable birds and the faint swish of the surf on the beach below, and with sudden determination Eden left the path and followed the bent grasses into the deeper shadow of the trees. She caught her breath as she passed some more red marks and then she halted abruptly at the edge of a small clearing when she saw a man collapsed in a kneeling position against a bush.

She ran forward and just as she reached him he slid to her feet, the gash on his temple filling her with dismay. Probably the best thing to do was to run back to Wayfarers for her father because she had nothing useful in her pocket but one very small handkerchief, but she couldn't just leave the man lying there full in a shaft of sunlight which came glancing through the trees.

She knelt down and pulled him gently into the shade, smoothing the black hair away from the cut. He moved restlessly, muttering, and she hesitated to leave him in case he came round and started crawling before she could get back with help. Now that she was close to him she could see that the injury looked worse than it really was, as it was mostly a flesh wound which hadn't gone deep. But it could cause slight concussion and it wouldn't help if he started wandering through the woods again.

'Keys,' he muttered. 'The lab – mus'n' leave – oh – poor ol' Roger—'

Eden held on to him as he jerked away from her, his eyes still closed and his brow furrowed with effort. 'Lab'? she wondered. Was *this* Justin Fontaine? The only description she remembered from David was that he had eyes of the deepest most startling blue, but all she could see right now was a thin pale face with black crescents of eyelashes beginning to quiver as consciousness returned.

'Wake up,' Eden whispered. 'I'm going for a doctor in a minute but I want to find you right here when we get back! Just keep still – you don't have to go anywhere yet.'

His breathing became less laboured and he lay still within her steadying protective arms. Slowly he opened his eyes, eyes so blue that Eden couldn't look away from them. He stared at her and then round the clearing as memory returned.

'Hallo,' he murmured, looking up at her again, and a faint smile touched the corner of his mouth. 'I thought at first – you were a small golden angel – that this was heaven—'

'Yes,' Eden replied dazedly, and without conscious thought she put her hand in his as he held it towards her and she trembled at his touch in the warmth of the morning.

TWO

'Who are you?' Justin Fontaine asked at last, his gaze travelling across her face like a caressing finger-tip. 'Visitors don't usually find their way in this direction.'

'Oh – I forgot you wouldn't be expecting us yet. You *are* Justin Fontaine, aren't you? I'm Eden Ashby and I just arrived this morning with my father and David Meredith and Nell Macgregor. We were waiting for the coastal steamer at Araquilla and then we got the chance of coming over on Clyde Dinsmore's yacht today.'

'No, wait,' he urged as Eden started to rise to her feet. 'You said something about a doctor, but I don't want one. Tell me, what's Dinsmore coming here for? Or perhaps he didn't say?'

'Well, as far as I know he's just coming to stay with a friend of his, Paul Randolph. Do you know him?'

'Randolph,' he repeated, and his mouth firmed. 'Yes, I know him quite well although I haven't seen him for some time. I've heard of Dinsmore too and I don't – oh well, it doesn't matter. Could you stand there while I get up? So that I don't fall flat on my face again!'

'Please let me get my father,' Eden pleaded. 'The bleeding has stopped but an injury there could be serious. How did it happen anyway?'

'I was just going into the lab,' he said as he stood up and leaned against a tree, 'but someone was there before me and I got knocked out before I saw who it was. Were you going anywhere special? I mean, if it wouldn't be a bother I'd be grateful if you'd come with me. David said in one of his letters that you helped your father in the mission dispensary, and maybe you could clean this scratch up a bit. I'd rather people didn't know about this episode.'

'All right,' Eden said doubtfully. 'It's rather more than a scratch and if it's worse than I think it is then you'll have to let my father look at it later. Is that all you're going to do about this attack? Keep quiet about it?'

He stood away from the tree and put his hand through her proffered arm, both of them standing very still for a moment as if this fresh contact robbed them of speech and movement. As indeed it had as far as Eden was concerned. She was vaguely aware of the sun-dappled path in front of them, but the touch of this man's slender fingers on her bare arm sent the blood racing through her veins like wildfire. Nothing in her life had prepared her for a moment like this and she was afraid to look up because she knew that the singing and the glory she felt inside must be reflected in her face. Suddenly she remembered that her companion badly needed attention and with a catch of her breath she turned to him, only to find that he was looking at her with almost transparent delight.

'Let's get you into the shade,' she managed, and they walked on slowly. 'You were saying – about this attack—'

'I know the reason for it,' he told her, 'and if I don't mention it I'd rather like to see if anyone else does, because I don't know *who* was responsible. My keys were still in my hand when I came round, so someone has managed to make a duplicate and I'll have to change the lock. Whoever did it didn't find what they were searching for, because if they had I would be better dead from their point of view.'

Eden stared at him, appalled, and his hand tightened on her arm.

'It's all right, Eden – and I'm not going to start calling you "Miss Ashby" now! – I'm on my guard and I won't be caught like this again. I should have guessed from what happened to a friend of mine that the – the thing in my possession would interest a lot of odd characters.'

'But what *is* it?' Eden inquired. 'Or shouldn't I ask?'

The path started to slope downwards and at the foot she saw a single-storey building with a red roof.

'The lab,' Justin said, and then he sighed sharply. 'I've never mentioned this business to anyone but now I shall have to talk about it. I need another opinion and I need to clear my own mind about it too. When we've finished with the first-aid box I'd like to tell you – if you'll be good enough to listen.'

'Of course I will. I'm consumed with curiosity now!'

She stood beside him as he unlocked the door and they waited just inside while he looked swiftly round.

'I was supposed to be out dolphin-fishing this morning,' he said, 'so it must have been a nasty surprise for the searcher when I decided to work instead! I was trying to make my way home when you found me but I'm glad I didn't. There would have been such a fuss and bother.'

'And the thing the searcher was after?'

'Here.' He held out the bunch of keys, separating one which looked old and a bit rusty and which had 'Summer House' scratched on its shank.

'It's hollow,' he said, 'like all these old-type keys, and the perfect hiding-place for a small piece of film. I looked at it when my head stopped spinning and I saw that the stopper of fluff and tobacco grains was still in the opening – it took me longer to make an innocent-looking stopper than it did to put the film inside!'

'All very cloak-and-dagger,' Eden said with a smile. 'Now where's your first-aid box? I'm dying to know all about this film, but you've been far too long without attention already. What's the water like in this place?'

He closed the door behind them and she made him sit down while she laid out lint and disinfectant and put a small pan of water on the electric ring.

'Who is Roger?' she asked as she swabbed the cut. 'You mentioned him before you became conscious.'

'He's part of the story and – and he's dead. You see, about a year ago I started experimenting with insecticides and I remembered something similar which Roger and I had worked on together in Florida. We did it in our spare time and in the end we gave it up as we didn't seem to be getting far. Since I came back here to work I intensified that kind of research and I knew I was on the verge of discovering something quite revolutionary in that line. Talk about playing with fire! What I got was a paralysing gas which would make the Department of Biological Warfare go off their heads with delight!'

'You mean it could be used as a weapon in war? Something like that ghastly germ-spreading idea scientists keep talking about?

'That's right.' His voice was harsh and he moved restlessly under her hands. 'Only my gas doesn't maim or kill. You could paralyse a whole nation with it and just walk in and take over the country without them being able to lift a finger. It's the most terrifying thing that's ever happened to me, and I don't know what to do about it. If I could discover this then someone else could do the same, so it's not going to help anyone if I just destroy the invention and try to forget it. What I'm doing now is working on an antidote, because you can't let a dreadful thing like this loose on the world without being able to combat it too.'

'Yes,' Eden said thoughtfully. 'The conquering armies would need the antidote, wouldn't they? Heavens, what an awful responsibility for you! Look, you must have a dressing on this cut, so you won't be able to pretend it never happened. Don't you think you should just forget the idea of trying to trap whoever knocked you out? Get police protection, hand your gas over to the government and then go on working at the antidote. Have you any idea who else is after it, and how did they hear about it anyway?'

Before he went on with his story he agreed that he must have a small dressing on his temple, and Eden bent over the crisp black hair and put a plaster on with gentle fingers. She closed the first-aid box reluctantly, feeling that there ought to be much more she could do for Justin Fontaine, but she smiled back at him as he thanked her for her help and then she sat beside him at the bench and waited for him to tell her more.

'I don't *want* to hand this weapon over to any government in the world,' he said with deep conviction, 'but I guess I'll have to do it once I've found the antidote. As for who else is after it, it could be anyone – a man who owes loyalty to no country and who is willing to sell to the highest bidder, or a potential enemy of the West, or even an agent from one of the Latin American countries where they're for ever having revolutions and government upheavals. And I'm afraid they found out through poor old Roger because he was the only other person who knew about it.'

The sun rose to its zenith, a mocking bird called impatiently from the grove outside the building, and Eden sat absorbed, having forgotten all about Wayfarers and the three who would be wondering what had happened to her.

Justin had been working on his new insecticide one afternoon and having just added the last item on his formula he became aware of a deadly lethargy in all his limbs. He had the presence of mind to shut off the vapour and dismantle his apparatus at once, but after that he was helpless for almost two hours. His mind started to clear before his limbs would function and he realized that a rocking sensation was due to having his shoulders shaken by Kara Brandt who had come down to see why he was so late for a cocktail party at Dayspring. She was talking urgently but he couldn't hear her, and when she turned and rushed out of the lab he guessed that she was going for help.

He knew then what had happened to him and why, and with the effort of his life he managed to place the results of his experiments and all his notes in a drawer. He had just locked the drawer and put his keys away when Dr Brandt hurried in with his daughter, both of them greatly relieved to find him almost normal. He explained that he had tried out a new malarial drug and that its effects had been rather more than he had bargained for, and with outward penitence he endured a lecture from Dr Brandt on the dangers of such experimentation.

He slept very little that night, and at dawn he was back in the lab checking and cross-checking his 'insecticide', at last having to believe what he had been afraid to admit to himself the evening before – that he had discovered one of the most potent weapons of biological warfare known to man. It was too big a thing to handle alone and he wrote at once to Roger, reminding him of their previous experiment and hinting in their own scientific code of what he had added to the old formula. It was almost a week before he had an excited cable from Roger to say he was coming to Caravel within a few days, so Justin settled down to wait and to wonder what Roger would suggest about the eventual disposal of the formula.

'He never got here,' Justin said, staring absently at the motes dancing in a shaft of sunlight. 'He was run down and killed by a hit-and-run driver in Miami when he was on the way to catch a plane to Trinidad. He was rushed to hospital by people who were passing in another car, but it was too late. Apart from our interests he was my oldest friend and it was a dreadful shock to me to hear that he was dead, but it was the kind of accident that could happen to anyone. Or so I thought until a couple of days later when I got a letter he had posted before he left for the airport. He said that his imagination had probably gone wild but he had the feeling that he was being watched, and so he decided that a piece of miniature film was safer than a page of notes. He had had a new idea which would make the production of our formula much easier and so he had written the whole thing and photographed it himself. He said in his funny way that planes had been known to come down in the sea and that if he didn't get to Caravel at least a letter might arrive by another route.'

'So then you felt that it wasn't premonition on his part?'

'I think he was afraid of something definite,' Justin said soberly. 'Perhaps not definite enough to mention in the letter, but he sent the film just to be on the safe side. So that's the story, and bless you for listening to it. Since I've been talking to you I'm more sure than ever that I mustn't let this thing out of my hands until I've found the antidote to it.'

'But someone has obviously connected you with Roger and it seems to me that you're in real danger! You can't guard your formula if you're dead! Oh, Justin, please get rid of that film – send it to Washington or London and trust them not to open it until you say they can!'

He shook his head stubbornly. 'The balance of power is such these days that any country would shout aloud if they possessed anything like this gas. They'd call it a deterrent and say they were contributing to peace by holding it as a threat over the heads of other nations. At the moment it's my responsibility and mine alone and it's better that way.'

Eden recognized the deep-rooted aversion to destructive weapons which David had mentioned, and she saw that it went far enough to make Justin believe that he alone was the best and only suitable guardian for this new and dreadful gas. She sat silent, wondering how to put into words her feeling that he must either destroy and forget this formula or else hand it over to a responsible government department.

'There's one thing I will do, though,' Justin said, removing the small plug from the end of the key and fishing out the film. 'One half of this formula is no good without the other, so if I keep them in separate places I double the chances of hanging on to it until I'm ready to hand it over. It's very complicated and I must keep a written record of it somewhere, not being blessed with a photographic memory!'

'The absent-minded professor,' Eden said with a smile,

watching as he examined the inch of film and then cut it carefully almost in half.

'I'm afraid I've been dreadfully thoughtless,' he said, putting the film down and looking at her with troubled eyes. 'This whole business so bothered me that I didn't realize I was giving you dangerous knowledge. Somehow I knew that you would never mention it to anyone, but now I wish I hadn't laid such a burden on you.'

'Please don't feel like that,' Eden said softly. 'I'm honoured to have your confidence and I'm glad if it helped you even a little bit to talk to someone about it.'

He finished pushing the larger piece of film into the shank of the old key and then he reached across the bench and placed a hand on hers.

'You've been wonderful,' he told her, and once more a wild joy ran through her body. 'I'm so glad you came—'

He stopped speaking as footsteps pounded on the path outside and someone knocked loudly, calling: 'Anyone there?'

Recent habits had made Justin lock the door when they came in and now he pushed the small plug into the end of the key as Eden opened her gold medallion and slipped the second half of the film inside.

'No!' Justin protested, catching her wrist even as the medallion dropped back beneath her dress. 'I won't have you mixed up in this to such an extent—'

She whirled away from him and opened the first-aid box again. 'You must! Now open that door – I think that was David's voice – I'd forgotten all about him!'

There was no reason to feel so guilty, she thought as Justin went towards the door, but the colour rose in her cheeks and her hands shook as she tumbled bandages and ointment on to the bench and then made a show of replacing them tidily.

David greeted Justin almost perfunctorily and then

stared beyond him to where Eden was rolling a bandage with brisk competence.

'What *have* you been doing?' he demanded. 'You've been gone for ages and we were worried stiff!'

He turned to look back up the path, and as he called: 'It's all right, she's here,' Dr Ashby hurried into view.

'Really, Eden, this is most thoughtless of you,' the doctor said angrily. 'You might have known we should worry if you stayed away like this the minute we came—'

'I'm so sorry,' Justin broke in. 'It's all my fault. I had a – a fall this morning and Eden – Miss Ashby – was kind enough to render first aid. We didn't realize how quickly the time was passing—'

Worse and worse, thought Eden, as David's eyebrows rose and her father glanced at her sharply.

'Father, this is Mr Fontaine. Justin, my father Dr Ashby. I'm very sorry if I gave you all a fright but it never occurred to me that anyone would think my absence odd. I went for a stroll and then I met Justin, and as he'd had rather a nasty fall we came here to clean him up a bit.'

'That's what I mean,' her father snapped. 'It could have been you! If you had fallen over the rocks or down a hole it might have been long enough before we found you!'

Eden smiled at him and cleared away the bowl of reddened water she had used. 'But it wasn't I, so we needn't worry any more. I nearly ran to get you but I decided that the injury wasn't serious and that I could manage alone. David, did you get the keys?'

'M'm? Keys? Oh yes. I got them from Joel who's the unofficial "boss" of Dayspring. He's gone to round up some domestic staff for us now. Been with you a long time, hasn't he, Justin?'

'All my life,' Justin said with a reminiscent smile. 'But your staff will be a bit "scratch" on your first day so please dine with us at Dayspring this evening. Kara will be delighted to have some feminine company for a change.'

'Ah yes,' David said, and there was curiosity in the glance he gave the other man. 'I saw her this morning, and I must say she seems more efficient than ever.'

'She's certainly a very good housekeeper,' Justin murmured, taking the first-aid box from Eden and replacing it on its shelf. 'Her father is in charge of the hospital and it works out well for all of us – he lives at Dayspring and she looks after us both. May I tell her that we'll be having company this evening?'

'Yes, thank you,' Eden said quickly as her father frowned. 'It will give our staff time to get settled in and I don't really feel like starting to plan meals until tomorrow! Well, I'm longing to see the inside of Wayfarers so shall we get along there now?'

Justin locked the lab door behind them. 'I'll come to the house with you,' he said. 'As far as I know it's ready for visitors but I was going to send Joel and the servants down on the day before you arrived.'

He led the way along another path with Dr Ashby, and Eden walked behind with David.

'It didn't take you and Justin long to get on first-name terms,' David said with a little laugh. 'From what I remember of him he didn't used to be quite so forthcoming!'

'When you're stinging a cut with disinfectant,' Eden said lightly, 'and when you're telling a man to sit still so that you can get on with the job, you're apt to forget to call him Mr Fontaine every time! Anyway, it's not as if we were complete strangers, because through you he's heard of me as Eden and I've heard of him as Justin.'

David said nothing and Eden wondered with faint irritation why she felt compelled to explain things to him anyway. She guessed that he was disturbed by the lack of strangeness between herself and Justin, and Justin's halting explanation of their meeting certainly hadn't helped to dispel the sense of intrusion which both David and her father must have felt when they came to the lab.

Eden looked at the two figures in front of her, Justin almost a head taller than her father who was trudging along as if he still wasn't in the best of humours. Her heart skipped and steadied as her gaze lingered on the white plaster which was just visible at the edge of Justin's temple. If the person who had injured him had found what they wanted then Justin would certainly have been better dead from their point of view, and for a moment Eden visualized a world without him and knew that it would be an empty world for her.

How long was in since she had met him? An hour? Two hours? It didn't matter. Oh but this was ridiculous! How was it possible to know after such a short time that her life meant nothing, would never mean anything, unless Justin Fontaine was a part of it? And what was time after all? It had nothing to do with this certainty that she had met the man who would always mean more to her than any other man ever could.

Ahead of them Justin drew back a thickly flowering branch of cat's-claw creeper and held it while they passed by. The path was narrow and for a second blue eyes looked into brown, and Eden knew that for Justin too the morning had had an unbelievable enchanted quality.

They came to the edge of the small wood where the path strayed down to Wayfarers, and Eden stood admiring the view. The promontory was a most pleasant position for a house, and the riot of flowers in the gardens made a dazzling display above the sea which stretched deeply blue on three sides. When they started to walk towards the house Justin and Eden were several steps behind the other two.

'You must give me that piece of film,' he whispered urgently. 'I'll never have a moment's peace until it's out of your hands!'

'Well, I can't give it to you now! You have to keep it somewhere, nobody could ever guess that I have it, and on the whole can you think of a safer place?'

'That's not the point! I had no business to involve you in this at all – sheer selfishness on my part and you know it! Please, Eden, let me have the wretched thing back.'

She sighed. 'All right, but only when you can tell me that you've got an equally good hiding-place. You know, this medallion is said to have belonged to an Inca priestess, and I only discovered the little cavity by accident. I wonder what *she* kept inside it? I've worn it for years but this is the first time I've put anything in it.'

'Not even a tiny photograph?' he asked lightly. 'No memento, such as a rose petal from your first bouquet?'

She looked up at him and although his tone had been casual the expression in his eyes was not.

'Nothing ever mattered enough,' she told him, and the very sun seemed to go reeling round the sky as their hands touched and then clung together with fierce urgency.

Eden came down to earth in time to realize that she and Justin were once more the centre of attention. Her father and David were waiting by the terrace steps, Nell was standing by a pillar just above them, and beside her was a woman with silver-blonde hair worn in a thick plait around her head.

'I knew you'd be all right,' Nell said, bridging the awkwardness of the moment. 'This is the kind of island where time doesn't mean anything at all, but these men went rushing after you like a couple of wet hens! Eden, my dear, this is Miss Brandt who very kindly came down as soon as she knew we had arrived.'

While Nell was introduced to Justin, Eden shook hands with Kara Brandt, feeling suddenly insignificant beside this tall Austrian with the magnolia-white skin and pale blue expressionless eyes. The firm mouth was innocent of lipstick, and altogether the impression given was one of well-scrubbed wholesomeness and efficiency.

Her greeting was polite if not effusive and then she frowned and looked at the dressing on Justin's temple.

'Justin, what happened?' she asked anxiously. 'How did you injure your head?'

'I was dreaming of malaria bugs,' he said with a smile, 'and I wasn't looking where I was going! Don't worry, Kara, it's only a scratch and I'll have the plaster off tomorrow. I really came along here to see if there was anything I could do to help our friends to settle in—'

'Joel is seeing to everything,' she broke in, 'and I have just been through the house myself. You must let my father have a look at this injury, Justin. Fortunately, he will be home for lunch today, and I think he will say that you must not return to work afterwards.'

'I am going back to work,' Justin said firmly, 'and this evening we are having a dinner-party. If your father and Dr Zeitler are free I'm sure they would be delighted to meet our friends then.'

'Oh – yes, that will be very nice,' Kara said with a brief smile at Eden. 'Now if they will excuse us I think you ought to get out of this hot sun for a time, Justin. A fall is most upsetting to the nerves.'

Eden's gaze flew to Justin's face and her heart lurched as she saw the small frown of pain between his eyebrows. With her mission experience she ought to have insisted on a sedative and complete rest after a blow like he had

had, instead of letting him walk back here with them. As if he knew what she was thinking he shook his head almost imperceptibly.

'Thank you for being such an efficient Good Samaritan,' he said softly. 'Yes, Kara, I'm coming. We'll expect you all for eight o'clock then? David knows the way. *Au revoir.*'

Eden watched them walk up one of the paths towards the trees, her underlip caught between her teeth. It felt all wrong that Justin should be going anywhere without her, and then as he seemed about to look round Kara put a hand beneath his elbow and in another moment they were out of sight.

'Exit Brünhilde,' Nell said with a snort. 'My word, she's even bossier than I am!'

'There's no nonsense about her,' Dr Ashby said, his recent ill-humour quite evaporated. 'And she's no mere housekeeper, eh David? She's got her eye on Fontaine and she's the type who would keep a man in order!'

'Yes, they did look well together,' David said, and he sounded as if he didn't quite know what to make of the man who had greeted him as an old friend. 'She's a handsome wench, but a bit overpowering for my taste.'

Handsome? Eden looked stonily at their backs as she turned to go up the steps. Kara Brandt was as cold as a fish and most certainly *not* the woman for Justin Fontaine.

'Come and look over the house,' Nell said, tucking her arm through Eden's. 'It's none of our business if Mr Fontaine wants to play Siegfried to that blonde beauty!'

But he didn't want to, Eden thought, and then her eyes clouded. How could she be so sure that the morning's revelation had been as clear to Justin as it had been to her? Had she, perhaps, been reading too much into the words and actions of a man who was bound to be a bit light-headed after a blow such as he had received?

Now that he was no longer with her she felt bereft and chilled and suddenly uncertain.

THREE

ALL the bedrooms in Wayfarers faced the sea, and Eden chose one on the west side with windows looking across the water to the next promontory where the red-tiled roof of Dayspring appeared above the trees. It was a curious mixture of architectural styles, David had said, plantation colonial with white pillars at the front, almost Moorish with arched patios and mosaic paving at the back, and upstairs balconies of lacy black ironwork reminiscent of New Orleans. But time had mellowed the contrasts built on by Justin's forbears, and David said it had somehow become a serene and gracious house.

Eden sighed and moved away from the window. She would see Dayspring for herself in a little while and there was really no need for this feeling that was almost stage fright. But it rankled a bit to know that your bemused entranced state of mind must have been obvious to the man who had caused it, and to wonder if his instant response was a mere nebula of wishful thinking on your part.

There was a knock on the door and Nell came into the room.

'What are you wearing?' she asked. 'David said "glad

rags" because society here is even more conventional than Boston or London, but I'm afraid they'll have to put up with me in my old blue satin.'

'No one here has seen it,' Eden told her, 'and you've always looked magnificent in it. It was about the one great extravagance of your life but you must admit it's been worth it.'

Nell grinned reminiscently. 'I never thought I could look really "grande dame" until I saw myself in that gown. However, if we're going to entertain or be entertained much I'll have to get some other dresses made as well. When are you going to show your father the materials you bought?'

'Well, he rather looked at me sideways just now when David mentioned dressing for dinner! I told him I was prepared because I'd been shopping in Araquilla, and then I skipped before he could ask any more!'

There was another knock at the door and an attractive coloured girl came in.

'Howdy, ladies,' she said with a wide smile. 'I'm Beulah, and I've come to see if I can maid you. I'm real good with hair, and handy with a needle, and I'm your housemaid too.'

'Just the person I need,' Eden told her. 'Miss Macgregor can have you afterwards but right now I want to find something decent to wear to night. Want to have your hair done "real good", Nell?'

'No thank you,' Nell said, shaking her neat grey head. 'Plain and no nonsense, that's me. But Beulah can come in later in case I need hitching up anywhere. Good hunting!'

To the accompaniment of Beulah's admiring comments Eden unpacked her new dress materials and Beulah put away garments which didn't need pressing. Then she stood with a finger to her lip studying the green chiffon gown Eden had put out to wear.

'Really pretty,' Beulah murmured, 'but that gold stuff you got – now that sure is a knock-out.'

'But it's an Indian sari, and I can't very well make my first appearance in that!'

'It don't have to look like a sari, Miss Eden. You give me a needle and thread and I just catch it up here and there after you got it on and I tell you you sure look a treat. Howsomever, you maybe should keep it for a bigger affair than dinner at the big house though Miss Kara she always dresses real splendid in the evenings. What about this blue dress with the silver birds, Miss Eden? You got just the figure for it and it's kinda plain if that's what you want.'

'Plain!' Eden exclaimed, and looked again at the gown of larkspur-blue Chinese brocade. Yes, perhaps to Beulah with her traditional love of colour and swirling skirts the line of the dress was almost severe, but there was glory enough and to spare in the material itself.

'Miss Kara's wearing pink lace,' Beulah said, smoothing the blue and silver brocade, and Eden smiled to herself. It was obvious that Beulah wanted her ladies from Wayfarers to be no less stunning than Kara Brandt.

'All right,' Eden decided. 'I'll wear the brocade. It may be cool coming home later so I'll wear that parchment silk evening coat. Press it please, Beulah? It's rather ancient so watch it doesn't fall to bits!'

'Not yet it won't, Miss Eden. You got nice things and you look after them and if they suit you it don't matter how old they are. You go catch yourself a shower and everything'll be laid out ready for you.'

While she showered and changed Eden mentally reviewed her wardrobe and came to the conclusion that finding Kharama had been a godsend. The green chiffon dress and the evening coat had belonged to her mother, and because they had been stored in a little chest in Eden's room Dr Ashby had missed them when he was frenziedly removing every memory of his wife after her death. He probably wouldn't recognize them now, and there must have been very few opportunities for a doctor's wife to wear such clothes in a jungle mission.

Eden sighed as she thought how few opportunities there were for anything there – books and magazines and the radio had kept her and her father in touch with civilization, but had that been enough? Now, with her world in turmoil after one look at Justin Fontaine she began to wonder if she could be as naïve and unsophisticated as her father and David believed her to be.

Her fingers trembled slightly as she dropped the gold medallion inside her dress, and she was glad that the neckline was high enough to hide the chain as well. The sleeves were very wide, edged with silver and lined with heavy silken satin in larkspur blue, and there was a sash of the same material with a wide silver fringe at the ends.

Beulah brushed Eden's hair although there wasn't much she could do about arranging curls like little golden feathers which went whatever way they wanted to go.

'You sure look lovely,' Beulah said sincerely as she gave her charge a final inspection. 'I'm just going to see Miss Macgregor now – she's a proper lady in that satin dress of hers.'

Eden has discovered in conversation that to be a 'proper lady' constituted high praise from Beulah, and from her reservation rather than from what she said Eden got the impression that Beulah did not put Kara Brandt into such a category.

Dr Ashby and David were smoking on the veranda when Nell and Eden came out, and as both women wore cloaks there was no opportunity for comment on what they were wearing. The older couple walked ahead, and as David took Eden's arm to help her along the path she thought with faint wonder of the tumult which that same touch from Justin had aroused hours before.

Dayspring was about ten minutes' walk through the grounds which adjoined Wayfarers, and even approaching from the side instead of coming up the wide river, the house presented a gracious and elegant appearance. Lights streamed on to the terrace from all the tall ground-floor windows, and the white pillars of the portico seemed to demand the arrival of horse-carriages and crinolined ladies with gentlemen in ruffled shirts and dandyish waistcoats.

Kara Brandt and her father met them in the hall, and Kara made the introductions after apologizing for Justin's absence on the telephone. A call from Trinidad, she said, had come through just a few moments earlier, and he had had to take it although he had wished to be present when his guests arrived. Dr Brandt, white-haired and charming, took the two men with him while Kara led Eden and Nell to the first-floor gallery where richly carved doorways opened into the bedrooms.

Eden was eager to see the inside of the house but she couldn't help watching Kara who mounted the stairs so regally in front of her. Pink was a mistake for a woman as well-built as Kara Brandt, and it was too indefinite a colour against her pale blonde hair and white skin, but in spite of her lack of dress-sense she had a presence which was apt to make other women feel almost insignificant.

She waited with them in the guest-room while they shed their cloaks and took a final look in the mirror, and for a moment her gaze met Eden's in the tall pier-glass. The usually expressionless eyes seemed to widen a trifle as she looked at the slender figure in blue brocade, and although her manner was correct as always there was a faint frown on her brow as she led them to the head of the stairs.

The men were waiting in the hall below and Eden's nails curved into her palms as she saw Justin looking up at her. It was all there in his eyes, the unity and the wonder they had felt that morning, and she was hardly conscious of anyone else as she came down towards him.

'The sun and the moon have come to brighten our lives!' someone exclaimed jovially, and Eden bestowed a vague murmur on Dr Zeitler who beamed impartially on her and Kara.

'The sun and the stars and all the host of heaven,' Justin whispered as they all went towards the drawing-room. 'Oh, Eden, it's been such a long day! Tell me – I shouldn't ask – but, has it been long for you too?'

'The longest of my life,' she confessed, and his blue eyes seemed to blaze down into hers. 'This morning was so – so shattering that afterwards I couldn't believe it had really happened. I wanted this evening to come quickly and at the same time I was afraid—'

'Afraid that I couldn't feel the same?' he asked in a low intense voice. 'That thought has haunted me since I left you! That I might merely have slight concussion and that I had imagined your eyes held a love I never dreamed of, that it was only I who trembled when our fingers touched – like this.'

Unseen by the others who were strolling through the doorway his hand clasped hers and her fingers responded instantly.

'My love, my darling,' he whispered. 'Never forget that you are that to me – my love and my life.'

'I could never forget a moment of this whole day. Oh, Justin, dare we be so sure, so soon?'

He led her to a carved high-backed chair and then stood looking down at her.

'Darling Eden, if we were alone you would know how sure I am that I love you with all my heart. I chose my moment badly – you should have had moonlight and flowers and my arms around you, and instead of that we have a roomful of people making polite conversation!'

'But I'm glad you told me. Aren't you glad too – to know that I love you? And I do, so very much.'

He could only look at her but it was enough. David was crossing towards them, a servant was murmuring something to her about sherry or gin, and she strove to control her fast breathing as she smiled vaguely and accepted a glass full of amber liquid. She was blind and deaf to everything but Justin's near presence and it was an effort to focus on David when he joined them.

'You look wonderful,' he said with appreciation. 'I must say I'm beginning to think civilization is better than pottering among the ruins of the past! Unless of course I can persuade you to come on our next "dig"! Does Mexico appeal?'

'Mexico?' Eden sipped her sherry. 'I'm not a trained nurse but I can't imagine what Father would do without me at the mission. The wife of the present locum has some training but they'll be leaving as soon as we get back, and if I left too—'

She stopped suddenly realizing that if her love came to its natural conclusion she would be leaving her father anyway.

'You can't stay in the jungle for ever,' Justin said with a smile that was for her alone. 'Excuse me, I must go and talk to Miss Macgregor.'

David's gaze was thoughtful as it followed Justin across the room and then he looked back at Eden.

'Glamorous sort of place this, isn't it?' he asked with careful unconcern. 'There's something about these islands that turns one's sense of values upside-down — as if we were seeing everything through rose-coloured spectacles.'

'That's odd,' Eden said, amused and yet a little touched by his anxiety on her behalf. 'They don't affect me like that at all. I've never felt so sane and sensible and sure of myself before.'

'You haven't?' His voice was full of doubt and his pleasant face was still clouded as they went forward to the dining-room. Eden knew a momentary compunction because after all he had had reason to believe that she liked him quite a lot and now he couldn't help but sense the attraction which had flared between her and Justin. Then her sympathy vanished as she caught the exchange of glances between her father and David. They had set themselves up as self-appointed watchdogs from the moment they had come upon her and Justin in the lab, and she resented the imputation that she wasn't fit to look after herself. She resented even more their reserved attitude towards Justine Fontaine, no matter how altruistic their motives were.

She paused for an instant as she entered the dining-room, delighting in the effect of candlelight and cut crystal and white flowers reflected in the gleaming mahogany table.

'How lovely,' she murmured, and Kara inclined her head.

'Thank you, Miss Ashby. Will you sit here, please, and Miss Macgregor on the other side?'

Justin was at the head of the table with Nell on his right and Eden on his left. Dr Brandt was on Eden's other side, with Dr Zeitler opposite, and Kara was flanked by Dr Ashby and David. The food was beautifully cooked and served, and Eden glanced at Kara with respect. She certainly knew her job, and even in her unsuitable pink

49

lace she looked strangely effective and secure at the other end of Justin's table.

Conversation, general at first, narrowed to a discussion between Dr Ashby and Dr Brandt about their early training.

'Vienna,' Dr Ashby said longingly. 'It was once the dream of my life to work with some of your wonderful surgeons there. But you could go back now, couldn't you? I mean, the type of German who invaded Austria doesn't exist any more.'

'Could one really call them German?' Justin asked. 'The Nazis were an evil branch grafted on to Germany, but there were thousands of ordinary Germans who could never have behaved like the leaders of that country.'

'No?' Dr Brandt's voice was an alien rasping sound in the gracious room. 'You did not see the things which I saw, my friend. Germans or Nazis, it does not matter, they are all – how do you say it? – tarred with the same brush. Even in defeat they were thinking of the distant future, dreaming of being masters of the world, and they do not care what means they use to achieve this life-long ambition!'

He stared unseeingly at the banana which he had been peeling as if wondering how it had got on to his plate at all, and Kara smiled faintly at Dr Ashby.

'You must forgive my father's vehemence, please. I was ten when we fled from Austria just before the war and I also remember many things which are best forgotten. My mother died on that journey and it need not have happened if we had dared to come out of hiding with her. Dr Zeitler was with us and he also is convinced that it would be foolish to return to Europe now.'

Dr Zeitler, his round face unwontedly serious, nodded. 'Germans or Communists, they are all the same except that the Germans are better at getting what they want by underground methods. The Communists do not care how evil they appear to the rest of the world, but the Germans like to be well thought of while they pursue their own nationalist aims.'

'But you sound as if you would condemn a whole race,' David said in surprise. 'Isn't it possible that Germany has at last learned her lesson? After all, there have been very good Germans in the past – look at Mendelssohn, and even at Karl Marx whose doctrines were aimed to help the underdog at the time, and look at—'

'Zut!' Dr Brandt broke in impatiently. 'Germany cannot even take credit for them because they were Jews. No, I shall never believe that the leopard changes his spots. I am happy here, and here I shall stay, and none of us can ever forget our debt to Mr Fontaine for making this possible.'

A sudden smile illumined his pale face and Justin smiled back at him. The shadow of past cruelties was gone from the room, and Eden drew a sigh of relief. For a time it had seemed that the argument might gather momentum and end in fireworks from the volatile Austrians.

Coffee and liqueurs were served on the terrace at the rear of the house, and Eden found himself sharing a garden-couch with Kara and Dr Zeitler who were interested in the working of the medical mission in Guiana. The conversation flowed easily and she marvelled at her own composure whenever she glanced at the other group. Justin was on the edge of it, sitting smoking on the low stone balustrade, and although his face was shadowed by a moon-flower vine she knew to the tips of her fingers that he rarely looked away from her.

'Eden!' Nell called to her. 'Dr Brandt is interested in the Inca civilization. Are you wearing your necklace?'

Eden's heart missed a beat and then raced on. She had

hoped to keep the existence of the necklace as quiet as possible, but now there was nothing for it but to show it with as good grace as she could muster.

'It's my lucky piece,' she said lightly as she rose, 'and I've worn it ever since my old Indian friend gave it to me. It's inside my dress as it doesn't look at its best against blue and silver.'

She crossed the terrace quickly rather than let Dr Brandt came to her where the light from the room behind gave a good glow. He exclaimed in admiration when she took out the gold medallion and let it lie in the palm of her hand.

'Beautiful,' he murmured, 'truly beautiful. You will permit me to hold it? It is like touching the spirit of past centuries. Yes, Miss Macgregor, I believe you are right and that this is a genuine Inca jewel — such fine gold engraving on this symbol of the Sun God. You will never starve, Miss Ashby, while you have such a valuable possession!'

'I don't even want to have it valued,' Eden said as she dropped the chain back inside her dress, vaguely repelled by the coupling of its beauty with its worth. 'No matter what it was made of I would still wear it because it was Dyqui's "lucky charm" and he wanted me to have it.'

'But it gives one even more satisfaction to know that one possesses something of great value,' Kara persisted. 'It is certainly a fine medal but if it were mine I should like to know how much it was worth.'

Justin laughed. 'Probably only as much as a museum would pay you for it, and they are notoriously stingy and like to have items presented to them for nothing! I think you can take it, Eden, that your best bet if you wanted cash would be to sell it for the weight of the gold and I don't believe you would get enough to retire comfortably!'

Kara looked disappointed and lost interest, and as Nell opened her mouth to protest Eden gripped her elbow hard. Nell gave her a sharp glance and then said nothing, and Eden was glad to see her father look at his watch. Justin had cleverly dismissed the gold medallion as being of no great value and now it dropped from the conversation as the Wayfarer's party prepared to leave. Danger to Justin didn't come from within his own walls, but it was just as well that no one at all should suspect the existence of the secret cavity which hid the small strip of film.

'By the way,' Justin said as they were leaving the terrace, 'the beaches on all three sides of Wayfarers are good for swimming, and so is the one below this house. But whatever you do don't use the one between here and the hospital. It's not sandy like the others and you probably wouldn't like the look of it anyway, but if any of you are strong swimmers you might swim that way from the other beaches and you might miss the warning notices at the water's edge.'

'I remember,' David said ruefully. 'The Cockpit! I'd be food for the fishes long ago if Joel hadn't streaked into the water when he saw me swimming full speed past this house!'

'It's some sort of crevasse in the reef,' Justin explained to the newcomers, 'and the sea gets sucked down into it with terrific force. Quite big boats have gone down in that whirlpool, and a swimmer wouldn't have a hope. It's more like a deep swell than a rough sea and you get very little warning, but if you stand on the headland and look down you can see a patch of water much bluer than the surrounding water about two hundred yards out. That's the Cockpit, so give it a wide berth!'

'We shall indeed,' Nell nodded. 'Every paradise must have its serpent and I wondered when yours was going on turn up! Well, I'm no swimmer myself but Eden likes to shoot into the water at crack of dawn – to my mind a most uncivilized proceeding before breakfast!'

'Shocking!' Justin agreed with a twinkle, and in his quick glance towards her Eden read that he would be looking for her somewhere on the beach first thing in the morning.

He and Kara strolled towards Wayfarers with their guests, but either by accident or by design Eden and Justin were well separated by the rest of the party, and without being very obvious about it there was nothing they could do.

But it's too late to separate us now, Eden thought, and the words were like a song in her mind. It was too late in the very first moment, that moment she would recall with wonder for the rest of her days.

When Justin and Kara left them just above Wayfarers, Eden had that same sense of loss which she had experienced in the morning. It wasn't quite so poignant now, because she knew that Justin felt the same, but it was sharp enough to make her flinch inwardly when David held her arm in an affectionate grasp. It was as if she belonged to Justin body and soul, and she shrank from the touch of any other man.

When they were indoors her father spoke to her for the first time that evening.

'I had no wish to make our differences public and that is why I said nothing about that preposterous garment you chose to wear, but now that you have made your experiment you will please return to clothes more suitable to your age.'

'I'm nineteen,' Eden reminded him gently, 'and I'm afraid you'll have to let me wear what I like. I've gone

54

your way for thirteen of those years, so don't you think you owe me this much now?'

'You – you look like a Jezebel,' he said harshly, and whirled away from them and went out again into the night.

'*Do* I look like that?' Eden asked the other two, and David exclaimed: 'No! I never realized before how lovely you are!'

Nell shook her head sadly. 'Eden, my dear, when I first saw you in that gown it was like seeing your mother again. She adored that colour, and with her red-gold hair it made here seem like a gorgeous butterfly that had strayed into the mission by mistake. She looked wonderful in all the brilliant jewel colours of blue and green and yellow, and I believe that's why your father has always wanted you to wear white or cream. Your mother never liked them, and when you wear them the likeness isn't quite so poignant—'

'My looks, good or bad, are my own,' Eden said firmly, 'and I'm not just only a blurred copy of someone else! And all this "poignant" business of yours, Nell – don't you think it's time he stopped calling me things like "Jezebel" whenever I remind him of my mother? All right, she *was* an actress, but she wasn't necessarily a painted madam! I know you believe Father needs special consideration, but why don't you stand still one day and look at his attitude honestly? I don't think you'll like what you see. Well, here endeth the lesson, and I'm going up to remove my "preposterous garment".'

Later, as she was brushing her hair, Nell tapped and looked round the door.

'Should I throw my hat in first?' she asked with a grin, and Eden laughed at her.

'I come in peace,' Nell said, 'and anyway we never had a chance to discuss our evening. Mind if I perch on your bed? I liked the two doctors, didn't you? And what was the idea of pinching me when I was going to tell Justin Fontaine that he didn't know much about the value of anything like your necklace? I was really amazed that he could be so ignorant about it.'

'None of us can know everything,' Eden returned. 'I was just fed up with the continual harping on how much money I could get for my necklace. As if I cared! If it was worth thousands I suppose it would have to be insured for a fabulous sum and I'd have all the half-witted collectors in the world begging me to sell it to them, or else it would have to be kept in a bank strong-box and I'd never see it at all!'

'Well! I'm terribly sorry if I put my foot in things but I had no idea you wanted to keep it a secret. I've been so used to seeing it round your neck that I never dreamed you would mind showing it to anyone else.'

'I didn't really mind,' Eden said quickly. 'I'm sorry, Nell, I guess I'm tired or something to fly off the handle like that. It's – it's quite an effort entering society after years in the jungle!'

'You did it to the manner born,' Nell assured her. 'They *are* frightfully correct in island circles, don't you think? It's as if they must do everything as it has always been done "back home". Kara Brandt can't have much of a settled background of her own but certainly fits into this one.'

'Experiences like hers would have made her mature early. If she was ten when they ran from Vienna she must be over thirty now, and I imagine she started to fit into any background she could find as soon as they reached Lisbon. How dangerously exciting her life has been compared to mine!'

'Maybe your excitements will start any day now,' Nell said, and then she chuckled. 'Maybe Kara will set her cap at David and you'll have to come to his rescue! Good night, my dear, sleep well.'

Alone again, Eden slammed her hairbrush on to the dressing-table and her wide brown eyes were mutinous. She wanted to think over the events of this strangest of days, to drift to sleep on half-formed dreams of the next morning, but thronging the forefront of her mind was this – this conspiracy to drive her into David's arms. She knew from past experience that her father would merely consider her 'foolish' and unversed in the ways of the world if she told him she was in love with Justin Fontaine, and with Nell and David of the same opinion it wasn't going to be easy to convince any of them.

But in spite of her apprehension it was Justin who was in her mind when she finally fell asleep with a little smile curving her mouth.

She was awake almost as soon as the tropical dawn flushed the sky and she lay for a few moments listening to the bird chorus in the gardens. There was silence in the house itself as she got out of bed, dressed in a shirt and shorts over her swimsuit, and then tiptoed downstairs with her towelling wrap and sandals in her hand. She had a quick wash in the hall cloak-room, stood rigid for a second as her toothbrush and plastic beaker clattered to the tiled floor, but when there was no movement upstairs she quietly unlocked the outer doors and sped through the garden to the edge of the promontory. She looked down with a stab of disappointment at the bare white sands on each side, and then her heart lightened as she saw Justin step from the shade of the trees on the Dayspring side. He waved to her, and she ran through the palms to the path leading down to the beach, the only place she suddenly realized which couldn't be overlooked from the house.

He was coming across the sand towards her as she reached the foot of the path, and with heightened colour she slowed her headlong flight.

'Good morning, my darling,' he said softly, and held out his arms, and she dropped her wrap on the ground and went to him with glad assurance.

For a moment it was enough to cling together, to know the ecstasy of holding each other close, and then his lips claimed hers in a kiss which seemed to draw her very soul into his keeping.

'My dear love,' he murmured at last. 'Oh, Eden, did you ever guess it could be like this? Yesterday at this time I had never seen you, and now you're the centre of my whole life. It's as much as I can bear to let you out of my sight for ten minutes.'

'Some day – you won't have to,' Eden said breathlessly, and could say no more because his mouth was on hers again with tender desire.

And neither of them heard the shrill call of the mocking-bird or the pebble which rattled down the path from the garden above.

FOUR

EDEN drew back slightly after a few moments, and Justin smiled down at her flushed cheeks.

'Beautiful,' he murmured, and then retrieved her towelling wrap from the sand. 'Let's go and sit in the shade of the trees – you can stay for a little while?'

'Yes, I think so, but I'll have to go into the water later

in case anyone starts wondering where I am! Justin, I – I've somehow got the creeps, as if we're not alone here. I wanted to look behind me even when I was in your arms.'

He bent to kiss her quickly as they walked into the shade of the palm trees fringing the shore. 'Nerves, my darling. I was here a good ten minutes before you arrived and I spent the time in having a scout around the wood. I didn't really expect anyone else to be up so early, and I was just playing safe. I know what's wrong with you – it's that wretched piece of film you're carrying around. Please, sweetheart, you must let me have it. I won't be able to concentrate on anything while I'm worrying about you.'

'Oh, Justin, no one could possibly know you gave me the film – all right, I took it from you – but they couldn't know about its hiding-place either. If I gave it to you now you'd have to carry it around until you found another safe place, and it's not worth the risk—'

She turned her head sharply and looked up the hillside through the thinly growing palms.

'Did you hear something?' Justin asked, and then he looked at her with concern. 'Why, you're shivering! Stay here and I'll have a quick search up there.'

'No!' She clutched his arm and held him back. 'I didn't hear anything, but I don't want you to go hunting among the trees. Remember what happened to you yesterday! Oh dear, it's probably nerves, just as you said. I'm afraid for you, and in addition my father is going to raise the roof when he knows I've fallen in love with you. He'll insist that I'm only a "babe" of nineteen, that I can't possibly know my own mind so soon, and the idea of marrying—'

Once more she flushed a deep rose under her tan as it struck her that Justin hadn't mentioned marriage and that she might be taking too much for granted. He laughed softly, with understanding, and drew her down to sit beside him under a palm tree.

'Eden, my darling, he'll just have to get used to the idea because you'll be my wife before the time comes for you to leave the island. It's hard enough now having you just next door but I don't know what I should do if you went back to Guiana even for a short while. I love you every way there is, we were meant for each other from the beginning of time, and we knew it within an hour of meeting. We've got something worth keeping – and worth fighting for if necessary. You do believe that, don't you?'

'Yes, oh yes,' she whispered against his cheek. 'But it's still wonderful that you feel the same as I do, and that you want me as much as I want you. Couldn't we keep it to ourselves for a while? Then when we do tell my father and – and the others they may think our feeling came gradually and they may not be so sticky about it.'

Justin smiled wryly. 'They're not blind, my sweet, and I'm afraid that our behaviour yesterday has already made them think very hard! When you say "they" I assume that you mean David as well as your father? I thought he was rather fond of you, and I'm sorry he had to choose you, because you're mine and no other man shall have you. But we'll try keeping quiet about it meanwhile – if you think it won't show in spite of ourselves!'

'It probably will,' Eden said, studying his thin tanned face. 'If you look at me in company as you're looking at me now – well, nobody could miss it! And whenever I look at you I feel all of a glow inside and it probably shows in my face.'

'And very becoming it is too! Darling, I think we'd better call it a day. If they find you've left the house they may decide to look for you on the beach. Same time tomorrow morning? I'll be working in the lab all day, because the sooner I can find the answer to my own horrible invention the sooner the whole business will be out of my hands. You don't really approve of my hanging on to the formula, do you? Well, I brought the thing into being and it's my responsibility to see that its use is safeguarded as much as possible.'

'I think you're taking needless risks by not trusting the Defence Department with it,' Eden said slowly. 'You may lose it altogether in the end, and lose your life too and that's what scares me more than anything. But, it's a matter of conscience with you and so I daren't say you're wrong. What will you do when you've got the answer? Send for someone, or post the formulae, or take them yourself?'

Justin's brow furrowed as he stared out at the sparkling water of the bay. 'I think I must take them myself somehow. The trouble is that we've no airfield, a once-weekly service with the outside world by steamer, and I'm not too keen on sailing my own launch to Trinidad. If only I knew which person or organization Roger became suspicious of before he was killed! If I'm under observation, setting off in a smallish boat with Joel isn't a very bright idea. But I'll think of something when I'm ready – oh, there's your father up on the path! 'Bye, my love. See you in the morning.'

They retreated farther into the shadows, held each other closely for a moment, and then Justin hurried away through the trees while Eden slipped off her shirt and shorts and ran down to the sea in her white swimsuit.

In a way she was glad of the interruption because it meant that Justin had forgotten to mention the film again, but she eyed her father warily as she swam out in the bay. He returned her wave of greeting and then went to sit in the shade near her clothes, and when she joined him he was smoking his pipe with lazy enjoyment.

'Breakfast will soon be ready,' he said. 'The other two are discussing their report for the geographical society and I think they mean to start on it today.'

'Oh. I half expected David to come down for a swim. Didn't he get up in time?'

'We're not all early birds like you. We guessed you'd gone swimming and as the coffee smelled rather good I strolled out to look for you.'

Eden glanced thoughtfully up the hillside while she dried and dressed herself. If the whole family had been together then her imagination must have been working overtime when she sensed alien eyes watching her with Justin. Of course, the whole situation was enough to make any girl start seeing things that weren't there, what with unknown assailants on the outside, and family friction looming ahead on the inside.

Breakfast in the cool shaded dining-room was a pleasant if quiet meal. Nell and David were mulling over their report, evidently deciding that it was best to get it out of the way as soon as possible and then to relax once it was written and dispatched. Dr Ashby was reading a week-old English newspaper, and Eden was wondering with faint self-mockery how she could get through the days on this island paradise if she could only see the man she loved for a few minutes now and again.

Later in the morning she was strolling through the gardens admiring the glorious profusion of leaf and blossom when a tall West Indian in a white shirt and denims came towards her.

'Fine morning, ma'am,' he said with a wide smile. 'I'm Joel Armstrong, and Mr Justin he calls me his right hand! I guess I'm a bit of everything from gardener to houseman!'

Eden held out her hand. 'I'm very pleased to meet you Joel. Mr Justin told me you more or less grew up together.'

Joel wiped his hand quickly on his denims and made a quaint little bow as he touched Eden's fingers. His coffee-coloured skin gleamed in the sunlight and his dark eyes were lively and intelligent.

'You'll be Miss Eden Ashby, ma'am? I have to thank you for taking care of Mr Justin yesterday morning. That sure was a nasty cut he came up with.'

He glanced over to the veranda where Dr Ashby was sitting with a book and then he looked back at Eden and the smile was gone from his face.

'He told everyone it was a fall, Miss Eden,' he said in a low voice. 'Now I don't understand that because he's even more sure-footed than I am and that's saying something. I been feeling lately that Mr Justin's in some sort of trouble, but I can't ask him to his face. Miss Eden – I'd lay down my life for him and he knows it, but this one time he's keeping close about whatever's bothering him and I sure am worried. I wouldn't ask you this if it didn't matter so much to me, but – do *you* think he fell?'

Eden studied the anxious expression in his eyes and she bit her lip in indecision. This was Justin's oldest friend even if he was just an employee, and his master thought a great deal of him. He was trustworthy and loyal and intelligent, and altogether an ally worth having.

'No,' she said firmly, 'it wasn't a fall. He was attacked when he went into the lab and for his own good reasons he doesn't want it known. For heaven's sake, Joel, don't breathe a word of this to him or to anyone else! But you're nearer to him than I am and maybe you could keep a casual eye on him without his knowing it. I'm sorry I can't tell you what it's all about, but he's in danger and I don't think he's taking it seriously enough.'

'Maybe not,' Joel agreed, 'but I am! Thank you for telling me the truth, Miss Eden. I'll watch him all right, and he won't know it and neither will anyone else. I come to look over the gardens here most every day, so if there's anything to say you could find me here. If you're interested in flowers it won't seem odd for you to talk to the gardener. Good morning, ma'am, and thank you.'

He sketched a salute and went to snip the heads off an overblown tree-vine just as Dr Ashby strolled across the grass towards them. Eden glanced sideways at her father and wondered with irritation if she was imagining things again; it seemed to her that she hadn't been alone since she had come out of the water early in the morning.

After lunch Beulah showed her some dresses she had made and Eden decided that there was no point in looking farther for a dressmaker when Beulah was clever enough and so obviously willing to use her needle. So they spent the afternoon and most of the evening in discussing patterns, cutting-out, and tacking the materials which had come from Kharama's bazaar. They used the small sitting-room near the kitchen quarters, but even there Eden found that the other three members of the party were just out of earshot on the veranda outside.

'Big dance coming off soon at the Country Club,' Beulah said, her tones modified as if she too were aware of the watchdog atmosphere. 'Mr Justin he never used to go to any of them because he said he never had time, but since Miss Kara came he takes her now and again. Likely you'll be in the party next time so I'll fix up that gold cloth into a proper evening dress. Country Club dances are special and all the ladies wear the best they got, jewels and all.'

Eden doubted very much that her father could be pre-

vailed upon to attend the dance and it was highly un-
likely that he would let her go without him.

'What kind of people belong to the Club?' she asked.

'Oh, the planters and the people that just live on their
money and don't do anything, and the white police, and
the white staff from Government House, and sometimes
the Governor and his lady if it's a real big occasion.'

'In that case my gold tissue is clearly indicated,' Eden
said lightly. 'All right, Beulah, I think we've done enough
for today. You can machine these when you have time,
but I have enough to see me through the next few days
even if it's only a shirt and shorts. I'm going to be lazy
and just have a rest for this first week – time enough to
explore the island later.'

Over supper Eden watched Nell thoughtfully. The
older woman looked disgruntled and for a change she
seemed to have little to say. Perhaps she was sorting out
her report and her subsequent book in her mind, but that
didn't square with her impatient glances at the two men.
Next morning Eden guessed the reason for Nell's behaviour.

She had risen just after dawn and as she picked up her
towel and sandals she saw that her small clock pointed to
a quarter to six. Suddenly she tensed as a door opened
father along the passage and she stood very still trying to
identify the sounds that followed. Then there was a
knock on her door followed by David's cheerful voice.

'Wake up, lazybones! Coming for a swim? It's a gorgeous morning!'

'Yes, isn't it?' she snapped and swept her door open.
'*Good* morning, David! I'm all ready. Coming?'

He jumped at her lively exit from the room, and as
his fair skin flushed Eden went to the head of the stairs.
Her father was hurrying across the hall with a key in his
hand and after he had unlocked the front door he turned

round only to stop short when he saw his daughter watching him. Anger made her skin prickle but she took a deep breath and smiled without amusement.

'Been locking the stable door?' she asked sweetly, and her father's mouth firmed.

'It is not a subject for levity that you can't be trusted to behave as a decent girl should,' he told her. 'Spare a thought for my feelings when I was told that my daughter was lurking in the woods with a strange man!'

'What a *horrid* thing to say,' Eden managed in a shaking voice. 'You shouldn't listen to sneaky stories. Why didn't you ask me about it instead of locking up the house in case I went out before David managed to tag on as well? Do you expect me to ignore everyone I meet except for you three? And now may I go for my swim as my watchdog is with me?'

'Make the most of it,' Dr Ashby grated. 'It's very doubtful that we'll be staying on this island much longer!'

Eden gasped with shock as he passed her and went back upstairs and then she walked blindly out into the sunshine.

'You made it all sound much worse than it was,' David protested when he caught up with her. 'I wasn't being sneaky as you called it, but I heard you go out yesterday morning and decided I'd have a swim too. Then when I got near the top of the path I saw you and – Justin going into the wood. Well, I mean, anyone could have seen you and neither of you seemed to care!'

'I might have known it was you,' Eden said bitterly. 'I thought better of you, David, than that you would handle this in the way you have. Not a word out of any of you all day yesterday! You and Father just sat stewing over it and thinking of how clever you were going to be this morning! Oh! You make me sick, the pair of you!'

She slowed down so that he had to walk beside her,

making sure that Justin could see from below that she wasn't alone. This fracas had put paid to any hope of seeing him even for five minutes, but as he had said, they both had something worth keeping and worth fighting for if necessary.

'I didn't *tell* your father about it,' David said with dogged persistence. 'I just stood where I was and then suddenly your father was behind me and I'd blurted out that you were both down there and then he was off down the path!'

'Well, the damage is done now, but I wish you'd both realize that I can speak to other men without your permission! Why are you so peevish about a man who was once your friend?'

'Justin's a complete man-of-the-world and you've never met anyone like that before! I thought you were a bit bowled over by him yesterday but I remembered that you weren't used to seeing many men or even to seeing houses like Dayspring.'

'Don't preach,' said Eden shortly as she stepped on to the sand, recalling with a pang that this was where Justin had held out his arms to her the morning before. 'You make me sound like a jungle waif having her first sight of civilization, but the fact is that I've seen more of life than you ever have and probably ever will do.'

She made for the spot where she and Justin had sat before, and with a forlorn glance up the hillside she guessed that he had gone away as soon as he had caught sight of David. Then as she dropped her wrap she saw a gleam of scarlet at the base of a tree and she bent to pick up a spray of immortelle blossom. It was freshly cut and it certainly didn't belong to the beach area, and she knew that Justin must have brought it and then left it for her to find.

'Immortelle,' she murmured. 'Everlasting.'

That said about everything there was to say, and with a lighter heart she ran down the beach and plunged into the sparkling blue water. David swam and dived nearby but he made no attempt to discuss Justin any further. His boyish face was troubled and Eden would have felt sorrier for him if he hadn't acted as he had. He really did think it was all for her own good and that her father was right in trying to protect her from the world and from her own 'folly'. But he did have an axe to grind and that would make it easier for him to believe that whatever he did was dictated by concern for her welfare.

When they returned to the house Nell was sitting on the veranda, and Eden stood and looked at her.

'You knew what was going on yesterday,' she accused. 'Really, do you too think I'm a half-wit?'

'Not exactly,' Nell said coolly. 'And you needn't take your mood out on me, because I'm only an onlooker. I didn't approve of the way your father wanted to handle this matter, but he *is* your father and it wasn't for me to interfere. Nor did I approve of what you had been up to, so I just sat tight and said nothing.'

'I wasn't "up to" anything, Nell! You and Father thought it would be fine if David and I fell in love and you're both disappointed because we haven't. I'm sorry, but life doesn't work out to please everyone. I know what I'm doing, and if I like Justin, what of it?'

Nell shrugged. 'Oh, I grant you he's a charmer, and he's got the most wonderful eyes. But that isn't enough to make a woman throw her cap over the windmill as you seem intent on doing, and it bears out your father's misgivings over bringing you here. I'm surprised too that you'd want to get so friendly with a man who's the subject of scandal.'

Eden laughed shakily. 'Do you know, I'd forgotten all about that! It's so out of character for Justin to be a

68

Casanova that these nasty rumours just don't register with anyone who really knows him.'

'But *you* can't know him after so short a time, and you must admit that you are quite inexperienced as far as men—'

But Eden was gone, helpless tears running down her face as she realized how impossible it was to make any of them understand that she was fit to manage her own affairs.

She had half a mind to breakfast in her own room but knowing that she had to face her father sometime she squared her shoulders and went slowly downstairs. He was already in the dining-room and as she reached the bottom step she heard his voice.

'Just how well *do* you know this man?' he was asking querulously.

'I thought I knew him quite well once,' David said in reply. 'He's nine years older than I am but we seemed to get on rather well when I stayed here before. I didn't like the tales about him and his – his lady-friends but apart from that he was a decent enough type. Now – I just don't know.'

'He would be more generous to you than you are to him,' Eden said as she took her place at the table, and David looked at her in baffled exasperation.

'Enough,' Dr Ashby commanded. 'We are not having an unseemly brawl in addition to everything else. Eden, I want your promise not to have anything further to do with this man Fontaine if we are to stay on this island.'

'I can't give you such a promise, I'm afraid, and you'll find it difficult to take me away by force. But I will promise to "conduct myself in a proper manner" as you would put it. I hate this unpleasantness and it's all quite unnecessary if you would only grant me the freedom given to any other girl of my age. You seem unable to believe that I possess even a modicum of common sense, but it's my life you're playing about with and I have some say in what happens to me.'

'You'll end up like your mother!' Dr Ashby said in a tense voice, and the veins in his hands stood out in ridges. 'I've been afraid of this for years—'

'That you would end up by driving me away too?' Eden asked. 'I've never believed that Mother ran away for good because she was going back to the stage! She probably needed a rest from your narrow-minded attitude and if the car hadn't crashed and killed her she'd have come back!'

Dr Ashby stood up, his mouth working, and then he turned and left the room without another word.

'Phew!' Nell muttered, and then she stared at Eden. 'Have you really always thought that about your mother? That she wasn't really running away?'

'It's what I've always told myself,' Eden managed, her voice thick with tears. 'I've still got some of the lovely clothes she made for me when I was small, so much intricate embroidery that it must have taken her ages to make a dress. I never let Father know that I had them, or that I managed to save a photograph when he was burning them all. She was so sweet, not the kind of person who would run away unless life just got too much for her all of a sudden. You knew her, Nell. You must have been shocked when you heard she was gone.'

'Of course I was! But I've never questioned your father's story that she said in her letter she couldn't live without the theatre any more. You can't remember anything about it, so I don't see how you can question it either.'

'I just know, that's all,' Eden said stubbornly. 'Oh heavens, what a rotten start to a holiday we're having! David, didn't you say there were horses available? I'd like

70

to have a good ride to clear my brain, and no thank you, I don't want a bodyguard! If it will set your mind at rest, I know that Justin is working in his lab and I intend to go in entirely the opposite direction!'

David gave her a hurt, reproachful look as he went out, and Nell shook her head.

'Aren't you being a bit hard on him? He did see you first, and it's no fun wondering if you've been snatched from under his nose by a man he thought was his friend.'

'I was never his to be snatched away from him. Oh, Nell, he's so *young*! Young and a bit spoiled and not the kind of man I would ever care to lean on. Put him beside Justin and which would *you* choose?'

She went to change into riding clothes but not before she had seen Nell's thoughtful and then startled expression. Even Nell had to admit David's immaturity when he was compared to Justin.

There was no sign of any of them when she came down and found Joel waiting with a horse outside the gate.

'This is Turpin, Miss Eden. You'll find him quiet and nice-natured but he'll give you a good gallop if that's what you want. You going alone? Then if you keep to the road that runs past Dayspring you'll come to the ruins of an old sugar-mill and that's the start of Calabar Beach. Two miles of firm sand there will give you a fine ride. Miss Eden, shouldn't you wear a hat? You look kinda peaky this morning, that's for sure.'

'Thanks, Joel, I've got a scarf in my pocket if I need it. I guess I'm just a bit tired. I – I suppose Mr Justin is busy working this morning?'

He bent over the girth and his voice was expressionless as he said: 'Yes, ma'am. I saw him safe inside and I heard him turn the key. I'll be watching for him again at lunch.'

Eden mounted and rode off, her cheeks faintly pink as

71

she realized that Joel would have followed Justin to the beach that morning and drawn his own conclusions thereafter. Oh well, that didn't matter compared with the fact that Justin now had an unseen guardian to look after him.

She reined in outside Dayspring as this was the first time she had seen it from the front. Wrought-iron gates in a tall stone arch opened on to an avenue lined with tamarind trees, and at the far end the house itself gleamed white against a background of feathery palms.

Eden sighed as she rode on again. It was a beautiful house in a beautiful setting, and if all went well some day it would be her home. But 'some day' sounded so far in the future, and she wanted to live there with Justin now. It wasn't that she couldn't wait if she had to, but life was suddenly uncertain and rather frightening, making one grasp desperately at present happiness in case it was lost altogether.

Leading from the sugar-mill was a gentle slope down to Calabar Beach, and Eden breathed deeply of the wonderful air when she saw the long empty stretch of sand in front of her. She had been afraid that others might ride regularly there and that she might have to make conversation with friendly residents when all she wanted to do was to be alone and to gallop off the cloud of depression which the scene at the breakfast table had engendered.

She was just returning to her starting point after a heady race along the whole two miles of sand when she saw another rider approaching from the sugar-mill. Whoever it was travelled fast, and Turpin danced and sidestepped as Eden reined in and tried to turn back again.

Then the rider waved and Eden just stared as Justin wheeled his mount to a halt beside her.

'We've managed our few minutes together after all,'

he said gaily. 'I met Joel in the wood on my way to lunch and he said he'd just saddled Turpin for you, so I sent him for Le Noir and followed you by the back trail.'

He took Turpin's bridle along with Le Noir's and led the horses to a group of palms where he dismounted. He tied the animals while Eden sat watching him in a trance of contentment, and then he came round to her side and held out his arms.

'Come along,' he ordered, his eyes alight with laughter. 'You look like Patience on a monument!'

He helped her down and then held her fast, his cheek resting on the top of her head.

'This is all I've thought about since I left you yesterday morning,' he murmured. 'It was a shocking let-down when I saw David coming to the beach with you. What happened? Did he hear you get up and decide to go swimming too? And did you find the immortelle flower I left for you?'

Eden nodded, unable to look up as the memory of the family fracas swept over her and brought a lump to her throat.

'Justin – how old do you think I am?'

'I can't say I've thought about it, my sweet! Twenty? Twenty-one? Why should it matter?'

'Because I'm only nineteen,' she said against his shoulder. 'David saw us on the beach yesterday, now my father knows and he's furious about it, and – and you have to be twenty-one to marry without your parent's consent. The one thing I am sure of is that my father will never give his consent, so how can I become your wife before it's time to leave the island?'

She did look at him then, half-hoping that he might have some answer to this insuperable problem, but she saw instead the sudden dismay which dimmed his former light-hearted expression.

FIVE

'I NEVER gave a thought to the legal aspect,' Justin said at last. 'But we can't be kept apart for two years! Maybe I'm getting superstitious or something but I feel that if you leave here without me I'll never see you again. It's probably just a selfish reaction on my part because I'm in love for the first time in my life, but that's how it is. Are you *sure* your father won't relent? Here, come and sit down although we mustn't stay too long.'

He sat at the base of a tree and drew Eden into his arms and for a time they forgot the urgency of their problems as they kissed with an aching tenderness.

'I don't want to stop,' Justin said with a wry smile, 'but this isn't helping me to keep a clear head! Now, darling, if we were very good and behaved very properly why wouldn't your father let us marry if we asked him nicely?'

So Eden told him about her mother and what her flight and subsequent death had done to her father; about her own sheltered upbringing and her father's watchfulness in case she too 'went to the bad'; and about the scene at breakfast that morning when he had threatened to curtail their stay on the island unless she promised to stay away from Justin.

'I see,' Justin murmured. 'It's all much more complicated than I had realized. Well, we needn't flaunt our feelings in front of other people, so perhaps the idea of taking you away by force will die down. Do you mind if Joel knows about us? He could be useful by keeping us in touch when there's no other way, and he'll have to know sometime! As a last resort, my love, we can always go to law and I think I could show that I'm a substantial

74

citizen and that I'm a fit and proper person to look after you for the rest of your life!'

Eden caught her breath. 'Of course! I never thought of that. It might be unpleasant for everyone, but it seems as if it will be the only thing to do. Oh, darling, you're just like a city of refuge!'

'What a comparison!' he said with a low laugh. 'But I know what you mean, and I hope I'll always seem like that to you. Now I must get back before Kara sends out a search-party. You know, she's a darn good house-keeper but she runs her father's life like clockwork and she would like to do the same with mine and I really don't care for being regimented. How does a mere male explain to a woman like Kara that he prefers to come and go as he pleases in his own home?'

'He just tells her so!' Eden said indignantly. 'None of them would be here if it wasn't for you! How did it happen that the Brandts came to live at Dayspring any-way?'

'Yes, that was a mistake on my part. Rhody, my former housekeeper – she's engaged to Joel by the way – was very keen to take up nursing when the hospital was started. I didn't want to hold her back and at the time I thought it was a good idea when Dr Brandt suggested that Kara should take her place at Dayspring. She came daily for a while but it was awkward, and it was then I suggested that they both stay with me as she could hardly live-in with just the two of us in the house. But I'll end the arrangement somehow before long, and certainly before you come there as Mrs Fontaine!'

The assurance with which he spoke of her as 'Mrs Fontaine' brought peace to her heart for the first time that day, and the echo of his words stayed with her long after he had ridden away and she was cantering back to Wayfarers alone. It was enough to hold on to, even if she couldn't meet him for some time, and it was comforting to know that Joel would be a link between them in the days to come.

An uneasy peace reigned at Wayfarers for the rest of that week and for most of the next one, and Dr Ashby seemed to be on the way to forgetting his silent wrath and to be returning to his old watchful but fairly even manner. Eden had been careful not to go swimming or riding alone, and she had spent most of her time gardening or reading in a hammock within sight of the house. Nell was the only one who attempted to mention Justin's name, but Eden coolly changed the subject and left Nell looking frustrated and a bit curious. David had lost his troubled expression but his face told Eden that he was feeling relieved and coming to the conclusion that her 'penchant' for Justin had merely been the flash in the pan he had always said it was. Well, let them all think what they liked. She was playing for time now, and none of them knew of the daily letters which passed between her and Justin, with Joel as a delighted postman.

At the beginning of their third week on the island Dr Brandt came to invite them to see over the hospital.

'I think it will interest you as you run a small hospital at your mission,' he told Dr Ashby. 'Also, you may be able to give us some ideas and we may perhaps pass some on to you! Mr Fontaine spared nothing to make our hospital a model of its kind, and now there is no need for any sick person to be taken to Trinidad at the risk of their lives. I could wish that Mr Fontaine had devoted his great talents to medical research rather than to agriculture, for he is a brilliant scientist, quite brilliant.'

If they only knew, Eden thought! If they only knew of the formula of death and destruction she carried inside the gold medallion under her dress! Now for the first time she really shared the conflict in Justin's mind when he had discovered where his researches had led him; understood his hesitancy in handing his invention over to the Defence Department, and his bitter knowledge that he dare not destroy his work because a potential enemy could discover the same secret and it was imperative that democracy possess this ugly weapon first.

She looked up quickly as she realized that Dr Brandt was inviting her to join the party, and she smiled her acceptance after receiving a brusque nod from her father who still had no intention of letting her wander far from his supervision.

David had hired a car from Amberley for the duration of their stay and while he attended to oil and petrol Eden went to change into one of the dresses Beulah had made. She chose a plain sleeveless one in green silk the colour of tender new leaves, wore plaited straw sandals in natural shade, and carried a large straw hat to match. Her golden hair gleamed after a shampoo early that morning and she felt quite pleased with the general effect as she applied a clear red lipstick.

Nell, stocky but immaculate in white linen, surveyed Eden as they reached the head of the stairs.

'How *do* you do it?' she murmured. 'In my mind I'm quite sure you're younger than your years, inexperienced, almost untouched. And then you turn up looking as if you've modelled beautiful clothes for most of your life, and as if you could meet any situation at all. I begin to wonder if my picture of you is quite accurate. '

'It never was,' Eden said quietly. 'You've all cast me for the role of innocent waif and you can't see beyond it. But you will, some day.'

'Um. I have a feeling you may be right although at this minute you resemble the cat that swallowed the canary! I gather that the recent display of "dutiful daughter" won't last for ever?'

Eden laughed softly. 'Gather what you like, Nell! It has at least bought a semblance of peace at the price of my independence, and it was worth that to stop the talk of an early departure from Caravel. Come on, the car's waiting.'

A wide tree-lined drive from the main road up to the hospital, and there were already several cars parked in the shade.

'Must be visiting day,' David said, and then nodded towards a Daimler with a pennant flying on the bonnet. 'Someone from Government House too – maybe Lady Hatherley is on one of her fruit-and-flower visits!'

'Don't you like her?' Eden asked as they drew up.

'Oh, she's all right. I met her several times when I was last here and I found her a bit inquisitive and – well, forthright. Unsquashable, if you know what I mean.'

'Interesting,' Nell murmured. 'I should get on with her all right!'

Dr Brandt was waiting for them in the cool reception hall and he told them that Lady Hatherley was there but only to see one of the servants from Government House who had had her appendix removed. Then he led them on a tour of inspection starting with the wards and ending in the well-equipped laboratory. On the way through a corridor Eden had heard him address a coloured girl as 'Nurse Smith' and while the others walked on she put out a hand and asked: 'Nurse Rhody Smith?'

'That's right, ma am,' the girl beamed. 'You'll be Miss Eden? Joel told me all about you and I'm right glad to meet you. You enjoying yourself on our island?'

There was a twinkle in her lively dark eyes and Eden guessed that Joel had told her of his activities as messenger between herself and Justin.

'Yes, thank you,' Eden said demurely, and there was an

answering gleam in her eyes. 'How about you? Are you ever sorry you left Dayspring to become a nurse?'

'I'm not sorry that I became a nurse,' Rhody said slowly, the laughter gone from her expression, 'but I don't think I'll see my training through. I just don't belong here somehow. Oh, it's a fine place and we need it badly on Caravel, but I won't be sorry to marry Joel and settle down at Dayspring with him. Of course I can't expect to get my old job back now that Dr Brandt's daughter has it—'

'Don't be too sure of that. When you decide to leave here, there's no harm in asking Mr Justin if he would like to have you back, is there?'

'You think—?' Rhody began, and then took a deep breath. 'Yes, ma'am! I doubt I'd have had the nerve to ask him seeing I left him like I did, but now I sure will have a try. Your folks are waiting for you, Miss Eden. I hope this turns out to be the best holiday you ever had!'

She returned to her ward, her starched skirts rustling, and Eden walked on thoughtfully to where the rest of the party were standing by the laboratory door. If Rhody wanted to return as housekeeper at Dayspring there was a heaven-sent opportunity for sending Kara Brandt on her way. With many thanks, of course, because she did the job well, but she was becoming too securely entrenched at Dayspring and that wasn't a good thing for anybody.

'This is where we do our own small research on tropical diseases,' Dr Brandt explained as he ushered them inside, and even Nell whistled under her breath when she saw the gleaming scientific equipment, the cameras, the detailed enlarged prints of viruses, and all the neatly labelled drawers and cabinets. Dr Ashby almost rubbed his hands, and Dr Brandt smiled.

'I think my friend and I will "talk shop" for a while,'

he said. 'When the rest of you have had enough you may go through this other door and you will find yourselves in the gardens which are worth a visit.'

Eden was the first to leave after she had strolled round studying labelled specimens in glass cases and admiring the parade-ground order of everything in the room. She stood for a moment on the veranda and came to the conclusion that the gardens were almost as orderly as the laboratory. It wasn't easy to curtail the spread of tropical fruit and blossom but an effort had certainly been made to do so here. How much more beautiful the scene would have been if the flowering bushes and creepers had been left to riot in their own colourful way instead of being kept to an almost geometric pattern. At one end of the garden a magnificent stand of immortelle trees had been grown as a windbreak, and Eden made her way towards the shaded seat beneath them.

She leaned back looking dreamily up at the scarlet blossoms, wondering how Justin was getting on with his search for an antidote to his own invention. That was one thing he never dared to mention in his daily letters to her, and he hadn't been able to mention the piece of film she had either. She hoped he had stopped worrying about it, and came to the conclusion that he probably had, because it was surely the last place in which anyone would dream of finding it.

The sound of footsteps on the path made her sit up and she saw a lady in a flowered chiffon dress coming towards her. The lady also carried a parasol of white silk lined with pink, and the reflection was most becoming to her milk-and-roses complexion. Her hair was blonde turning silver and it was set off by a frothy confection of white tulle and rosebuds.

'My dear, how pretty you are,' she said, and then laughed as she closed her parasol and sat beside Eden. 'Do forgive me, but I saw you from the terrace and really I haven't seen such a picture for a long time. A woodland nymph, I told myself, and I half expected you to disappear before I reached you! I'm Lady Hatherley, and my husband is Governor of the Claremont group of islands.'

' "Caravel, Claremont, Culverin Quai",' Eden quoted, returning the infectious smile, ' "Constantine and Canzonet." I love that rhyme. I'm so pleased to meet you, Lady Hatherley. I'm Eden Ashby, and with my father and two friends we're holidaying at Wayfarers on Mr Fontaine's estate.'

'Ah, yes, I had heard that you were there. Mr Fontaine is a most delightful man, don't you think?'

Eden laughed aloud. Her companion's transparent interest was too genuine to be the mere 'inquisitiveness' with which David had charged her, and her mouth was gently curved and her grey eyes kind.

'I'm afraid I haven't seen very much of him,' Eden said, crossing her fingers unobtrusively. 'He – he works very hard, you know, and I seem to find plenty to keep me occupied at home.'

'Really?' Lady Hatherley murmured. 'The other two members of your party are archaeologists, I believe? How fascinating. Yes, I think I met Mr Meredith when he was here before – quite a pleasant young man. Miss Macgregor of course is known by reputation and I am told that she is rather brilliant in her own line. My husband will adore meeting her as he is quite mad about digging up the past and I'm afraid he finds me rather a nitwit about anything like that.'

'Really?' Eden echoed, and they laughed together like a couple of conspirators who knew well that all a man needed was the right woman in his life.

'Now,' said her ladyship, 'we must think about some

parties and picnics while you are here. Yes, the ball at the Country Club next week promises to be quite an occasion this time. Have you arranged to go already? With a Dayspring party perhaps?'

'Well, no, I don't think we'll be going with a party from there. You see, we – my father badly needed this holiday and he hasn't been keen on mixing with people. So we haven't seen much of anyone and I don't think he would care for the idea of us going to the ball.'

Lady Hatherley prodded the earth with the ferrule of her parasol for a thoughtful moment and then she turned to Eden with a brilliant smile.

'We'll get him there all right,' she said. 'Has he any vices like bridge or canasta or even poker?'

'Not one! He looks on cards as an invention of the devil, and the only one I could recognize is the Ace of Spades! But he's very fond of chess, and when he was overworking back at the mission that was the only way I could get him to relax – by getting out the set myself or else roping in one of the teachers to do it. But chess doesn't go with a ball at the Club!'

'No, but it goes with a nice quiet evening at Government House when the rest of us are at the ball! If only I can rope in Captain Ross who's quite the worst chess-fiend I know, it might tempt your father. He's a retired sea-captain and he says that no one on Caravel can give him a decent game. Why, I'd be doing them both a good turn if I brought them together, wouldn't I?'

'But of course!' Eden chuckled. 'What if Captain Ross has another engagement on the night of the ball?'

'He'll break it if I ask him nicely. He's a gallant old dear, and between me and the promise of a decent opponent for chess he'll cave in at once! Ah, here comes your family with Dr Brandt. Shall we go to meet them?'

Lady Hatherley was the eternal woman, Eden decided,

watching with affectionate amusement as her ladyship cast her toils about Dr Ashby's feet. The temptation she provided in the shape of Captain Ross was too much for the doctor's disinclination to mix with outsiders, and before he quite knew how it had happened he was engaged to play chess on the night of the ball.

'Splendid,' said her ladyship happily. 'We'll send a Daimler for the four of you and we'll have champagne and sandwiches at Government House first. I'm not asking you to dinner that evening as my husband is entertaining a trade delegation and the meal will be early and full of shop talk. So dull for you! But you must all come to dinner the following week – it would be a favour to us as we see so few new faces. Au revoir, then, until Friday.'

'I like her,' Nell stated in her forthright manner as soon as her ladyship had gone to her car escorted by Dr Brandt. 'Not a mean bone in her body as the saying goes.'

'She's a past mistress in the art of managing people,' Dr Ashby said ruefully. 'I really didn't want to start mixing with the Government House set.'

'Rubbish!' Nell snapped. 'It will do us all good to have a bit of fun, and I mean you too, Charles! You've lived far too long in the jungle, and it's Eden's right as a girl of nineteen that she should see some life at last. As for David and me – maybe her ladyship's champagne will wash away some of the dust of past centuries from our outlook!'

'Well!' David exclaimed as Nell strode in front of them to the car. 'What's come over her all of a sudden?'

'Civilization,' Eden said shortly. 'I imagine it hits you like a fever for which there's no inoculation, but it'll wear off. She'll be quite ready for Mexico when you are, but she'll have had a bit of a fling first and it will do her all the good in the world.'

'What about your own fever?' her father broke in

with a sharp look. 'You never gave me the promise I asked for, but your recent behaviour has been fairly normal.'

Normal! Eden thought of the hours spent sewing and reading and gardening where her every action could be seen, and she sighed over the gulf of misunderstanding between herself and her father. Then she smiled at him.

'The fever's quite gone,' she said truthfully, knowing that it had settled to a steady glow which would illumine the rest of her life. 'Now I want to have some fun, just like Nell, before work begins again.'

'Fair enough,' David said, beaming at her. 'We'll see that they both have it, won't we, sir?'

Dr Ashby grunted but he didn't seem ill-pleased, and although Eden felt her conscience give her a prod over her equivocal words she felt that the lightening of the atmosphere was well worth it.

She continued to be careful and to exhibit nothing but 'normal behaviour', but she ached for a sight of Justin as the days passed and she heard of him only through Joel. He had told her in one letter that he was taking Kara to the ball, but whether he and Eden would dance together would be in the lap of the gods.

On the Friday after early dinner Beulah went to Eden's room and they spread out the yards and yards of gold tissue.

'I know you don't want to cut this, Miss Eden, but you can easy spare about two yards for a stole and that would look smarter than your silk evening coat.'

Eden agreed, and then Beulah proceeded to drape the lovely fabric on her, holding it here and there with pins where she would later catch it together with invisible stitches.

'There, Miss Eden, that's how it'll look and don't it hang just perfect? You got plenty room round the foot, though when you're standing still it hangs soft and pretty like this. You want that I should cover both shoulders? I could do it that way but you got real nice skin and it don't hurt none to show it.'

Eden was standing in front of the long mirror looking doubtfully at her one bare shoulder. Beulah had skilfully draped the material so that it crossed fairly high at the back and front of the neck, but there was something almost pagan in the reflection that looked back at her. She didn't want to change an inch of Beulah's work, but *what* would her father say?

'We'll have it exactly like this,' she said rather breathlessly. 'You're a genius, Beulah, and I'm terribly grateful.'

'It's my pleasure, ma'am,' Beulah beamed, unwinding the yards of gold. 'You sure pay for dressing. I'll go make up the stole now because that's all that needs doing early. You know, Mr Justin he's got a little statue in his library and you look just like it. The woman's wearing flowing stuff like this and she seems to be running. All in marble it is, but you can almost believe her dress is real. Ata – something it's called.'

'Atalanta?' Eden asked, and Beulah nodded.

'That's it, ma'am. Now you have a rest until it's time to have your shower because you want to look as good as what you're wearing tonight.'

With which final admonition she went out, leaving Eden smiling faintly at the comparison with Atalanta who had made all her suitors run a race with her and who had promised to wed the one who could outrun her. It looked as if *this* Atalanta would have to go with her love and hope they could both outrun the pursuers.

After she was dressed Eden put on the jade ear-rings she had bought from Kharama and then stepped back to look at her reflection. Yes, she needed that touch of colour against the beauty of her dress and her Inca necklace, and the jade matched the green border of the fabric and was the same shade as her high-heeled sandals. Beulah was giving Nell a final inspection so Eden picked up her stole and went into the next room.

'Wow!' Beulah breathed, and Nell grinned.

'My dear Eden, you'll give your father a heart attack! You stay right here until the car is announced, because if you go down early he'll send you back to put on something sweet and simple! I decided to stick to my old blue because I feel so good in it and that's the main thing. Listen, is that the car now?'

'Yes, it is. You go first, Nell, and I'll be a few steps behind you just in case Father sees too much too soon! Thanks for sewing me into my dress, Beulah!'

'I'll unpick you when you come home, Miss Eden! I sure hope you both have a lovely time.'

Dr Ashby looked sharply at the golden figure of his daughter as she skipped smartly into the Daimler, but David murmured with a catch of his breath: 'Eden, you look wonderful!'

'Thank you,' she said, her brown eyes sparkling. 'You look pretty good in tropical kit yourself, although I must say I feel rather like Cinderella!'

The feeling persisted as she stepped out of the car at Government House and they went in to meet Sir Mungo and Lady Hatherley, the latter in turquoise chiffon and sapphires.

'We *are* a nice-looking lot,' her ladyship said with great satisfaction as the champagne came round. 'Dr Ashby, allow me to congratulate you on the ladies of your household. Captain Ross, don't you wish you were coming with us?'

'Much as I love you, my lady,' said the Captain, 'no. Who would want to tramp around a noisy ballroom when they could be sitting in silent contemplation of these beautiful ivory chessmen?'

'I don't know that you haven't got the best of the bargain after all,' Sir Mungo grumbled, and Dr Ashby murmured 'Hear, hear', with a fervour that made everyone laugh.

Eden breathed a sigh of relief. It seemed that the evening had got off to an excellent start and that her father was quite happy to leave her under Lady Hatherley's wing. How nice he could be when he stepped so occasionally from the shadows of the tragedy which had darkened his life.

They arrived at the Club about nine o'clock and after more introductions than Eden could sort out in her mind Lady Hatherley swept her and Nell to the elegant powder-room where they left their wraps. The two men were waiting for them in the hall where a few wide steps banked on each side with flowers and greenery led down to the ballroom.

As she reached the top of the steps Eden glanced quickly round the room until she saw Justin watching her from beside a pillar. Her heart raced as he gave her a faint smile and then Lady Hatherley touched her arm gently and they went down the steps and across to their table. The band was playing softly and people were moving about among the tables lining the walls, but Eden felt that the Government House party was the cynosure of all eyes and she touched her gold medallion fleetingly as if for reassurance. She was very much aware of Kara Brandt's narrowed stare – Kara who looked striking and Junoesque in peach satin but who could have looked almost beautiful in black had she but known it.

Eden had the first dance with David who looked just a little uncomfortable when they met Justin and Kara on the floor and exchanged greetings. But the two who meant so much to each other contented themselves with nods and a cool 'Good evening'.

When Eden had danced for the third time with one of the young men introduced by Lady Hatherley she frowned when she saw the haste with which David returned his pretty young partner to her friends and then came hurrying back to the table. She had noticed that even on the floor his gaze followed her constantly and she wondered with annoyance if it was Justin he was afraid of, or if he didn't like her to pay attention to any other man at all.

'You know you're "made" for the rest of your stay, don't you?' he asked ruefully as he sat down. 'With her ladyship taking such an obvious interest in you, every man in the place will be after an introduction.'

'Phoo!' Eden said with a careless shrug. 'Safety in numbers as Father would say! And don't forget it cuts both ways – you're in her party too so all the girls will be mad about a new male!'

She noticed someone wave from a few tables farther along and she smiled at Clyde Dinsmore as he got to his feet and bowed. He made no move to speak to her and she wondered if he had yet achieved his desired introduction to Justin Fontaine. Perhaps that was why he was here, so that she or David might perform it. Or perhaps he was just having a quiet holiday on the island and was loathe to leave it.

Before she could be claimed for the following dance Lady Hatherley appeared with Justin in tow.

'Justin dear,' she said, 'I know I promised you this dance but do forgive me and dance with Eden instead. The Secretary is almost having D.T.'s over a missing box of cigars for a spot prize and I just *know* that I brought it down this morning. I must straighten the muddle for the poor man – what *would* they do without women on the committee?'

Eden and Justin danced a foxtrot in silence for a time and then Justin murmured: 'She's a sweetheart, isn't she? One little word in her ear and she clears the decks for action! David thinks it's all her doing, and it was the only way to get you out from under his watchful eye!'

'Oh Justin, you didn't tell her about us?'

'She's an old friend and a good one, my sweet, and she adores a bit of intrigue. Besides, she told me she was terribly pleased about it and couldn't have done better if she'd made the match herself! But I had another reason for wanting to speak to you. You were right all along to tell me I was crazy to hang on to my formula, and although my recent experiments aren't finished I'm taking the whole thing to Washington tomorrow. The coastal steamer leaves early in the morning and I've booked a seat on the plane from Trinidad in the afternoon.'

'Oh darling, I'm so glad you're getting rid of the thing! Now I'll have to give you the film.'

She looked thoughtfully at Clyde Dinsmore who was dancing with his partner not far away.

'Justin, have you met Dinsmore yet? I always felt he was more interested in you than in anyone else here.'

He raised a quizzical eyebrow and looked down at her. 'Are you connecting him with my blow on the head? He's ruthless, I believe, but I doubt if he was responsible for that when he wasn't even here. That's his friend Randolph, by the way, dancing with Kara. He's rather smitten but she doesn't give him much encouragement. Now darling, the film. Could you go to the powder-room and slip it out of your necklace and then pass it to me later?'

Eden shot a glance at David who wasn't dancing and who was sitting at the table watching her all the time.

'That's almost a "petted lip" he's got,' she said crossly.

'If I go near you again this evening he and Father will put their heads together and we'll have the horrid suspicious time we had the first week. I'm trying to keep everything on an even keel until you get back from Washington so that when you do speak to Father we might be able to count on an atmosphere of sweet reason! I'll have to give you the whole necklace. You know how to get at the cavity? Press hard on the smooth back near the top and at the same time give a downward push and the back will slide off.'

The music died away and before she turned out of Justin's arm Eden gave a sharp tug at the medallion. The slender chain broke and she almost cried out as it cut into her neck, but it helped her to look dismayed.

'My chain's broken!' she cried, and caught the whole necklace as it was about to slide to the floor. 'Oh Justin, could you mend it for me? You've got all sorts of gadgets in your lab and I don't want to take it to a jeweller who might keep it for ages. Look, you'll have to take the whole thing because the chain's attached to those links at the back. Could you send Joel over with it? It's – it's my luck, you know.'

'I know,' he murmured under cover of the conversation all around them. 'Bless you, my love.'

He slipped it into his pocket just as David bent to have a closer look at it.

'You'll have it back first thing in the morning,' he promised. He nodded to David, spoke for a few minutes to her ladyship, and then returned to Kara Brandt.

'I could probably have mended that for you,' David said, nettled. 'There was no need to have given it to him.'

'D'you think I *want* to let it out of my hands?' she asked, feeling strange and comfortless without the necklace she had worn for so long. 'Justin has the facilities for mending it properly and that's better than an insecure job without tools! Really, David, must you be a dog-in-the-manger? Do you object to the fact that his servant will be returning it to me? I can't think of any other reason!'

'Of course I don't mind that! I – I'd forgotten Joel was to bring it back. I'm sorry, Eden, it's only that Justin is a much smoother character than I had remembered and I guess I don't quite trust him.'

Eden was saved from having to reply as Sir Mungo came to take them to the buffet which had been set up in the garden room. Nell and Lady Hatherley left the group where they had been discussing Mexico, and Nell raised her eyebrows when she saw Eden's set face.

'Trouble?' she asked. 'I suppose David didn't like your dancing with his one-time friend?'

'David just doesn't like his one-time friend, and if that isn't small-minded I don't know what is!'

Her neck was hurting where the chain had scraped it, she hated the way Kara Brandt seemed to flaunt possession of Justin as they came into the buffet, and she disliked the glint in Paul Randolph's eyes as he watched them. Altogether the evening had lost most of its enchantment, and it lost some more when she saw Randolph bring Clyde Dinsmore to Justin's table. She tried to watch them all unobtrusively but with David in her direct line of vision she had to pretend an interest in all the young men who looked hopefully at her when they came to speak to Lady Hatherley.

'Tired, my dear?' her ladyship asked as they returned to the ballroom. 'I think another couple of dances will be enough for us all. I'm so sorry you and Justin are meeting obstacles, but do remember that I'd love to help if I can, won't you?'

'I will,' Eden said gratefully. It helped to know that she had a strong ally in her ladyship, and she had come to the conclusion that Nell was on the way to being an ally too.

She could have had a full engagement-book for weeks but she parried invitations with a skill she hadn't known she possessed, and it was almost with relief that she said good night to the Hatherleys and sank into the comfortable back seat of the Daimler. No one else seemed to have noticed the disappearance of her necklace, and she kept her stole high round her neck when the car stopped at Government House to pick up her father. He was in good spirits, having found in Captain Ross an opponent worthy of his mettle although honours were fairly even during their first chess meeting.

'I enjoyed myself thoroughly,' he said when they were back at Wayfarers. 'Your dancing until this hour can't have done any of you much good! Eden, that dress was a bit daring for a young girl. I didn't realize until you removed that scarf thing at the Hatherleys that you had gone quite so far!'

'It just seems daring,' Eden said mildly. 'Lots of the women, including that "wholesome creature" Kara Brandt, had both shoulders, half their chests, and most of their backs bare!'

'True,' Nell murmured as they went upstairs together. 'But it's like a woman looking much more abandoned in a négligé than if she's wearing nothing at all! Well, there's Beulah waiting to unpick you. Don't you wish you had worn something sweet and simple after all? No, I'll bet you don't, not after hearing one of the Governor's aides describe you as a golden goddess!'

She grinned and went to her room, leaving Eden to think about the morning and Justin's errand and to hope that he would get away without the wrong people knowing he was gone.

Before she went down to breakfast she heard the ship's

siren in the distance and she waited with concealed impatience until she saw Joel strolling through the garden with his sécateurs.

'Hallo, Joel,' she said, crossing the grass. 'Did you bring my necklace?'

'Sure did, ma'am, and here it is as good as new. Miss Eden – I was to drive Mr Justin to the boat but he never came, and then one of the maids told me he was real sick and couldn't raise his head off the pillow!'

SIX

'CAN you find out how bad this attack is?' Eden asked anxiously. 'I mean, what *is* it anyway?'

'I sure aim to find out, Miss Eden, but I came to tell you as soon as I knew I'd find you out here. I did hear Miss Kara say something about a kind of fever, but whether she meant fever of the blood or the kind that you catch like malaria, I don't know. Could you maybe do some gardening this morning and I'll come back with some seeds we been talking about? I'll go and ask to see Mr Justin – I'm his man and I got a right to know about him even if Miss Kara don't like to have me working indoors.'

Eden picked up his basket and sécateurs and went round the gardens cutting off overblown blossoms and she wasn't surprised when she found herself cutting away buds and everything else. All her fears for Justin's safety had been partly set at rest by his decision to go to Washington at once, but now they returned with redoubled force and made her heart race unevenly. Suddenly she thought of the film and in the shade of a bush she knelt down and opened her medallion. The film was gone, so Justin must have taken it the night before when he had mended the chain. But where was it now? If he expected to leave early in the morning he might not have been able to put it in as safe a place as her necklace, and what would happen now that he was too ill 'to raise his head off the pillow'?

Although she longed to run to Dayspring to get news at first-hand, she made herself stay in sight of the house where her father was writing and where Nell and David were putting the finishing touches to their report for the geographical society. She couldn't do any good at Dayspring and it would only cause the family upheaval which she and Justin were trying to avoid.

Her hands were busy among luxurious weeds in a flower-bed and her gaze was fixed and unseeing when Joel returned with his seeds and knelt down beside her.

'I saw him,' he said in a low voice. 'He's sick right enough but he says it's not natural and that someone must have slipped him a drug in what he ate or drank last night. Miss Eden, things like this haven't ever happened before. I'm scared.'

'Heavens above, so am I! How could anyone possibly know he planned to leave this morning? He didn't tell a soul except you and me.'

'He wants to see you, Miss Eden, if we can manage it. Dr Brandt said he'd been overworking and he'd had a return of the fever he caught in Guadalcanal at the end of the war, and Mr Justin he didn't argue about it. Miss Kara's going to the hospital with her father for some medicine and while they're away we could maybe get you up the veranda stairs for a few minutes.'

'What a mess,' Eden thought as she still knelt on the grass. 'I have the right to be with him when he's ill but I have to lie and cheat and creep up the back stairs!'

She stood up and dusted her hands.

'Saddle Turpin for me please, Joel,' she said clearly. 'I'm full of cobwebs this morning and I want to blow them away!'

He went to do her bidding and as she reached the veranda David asked eagerly: 'Want some company? I could do with some wind in my face too!'

After looking up from her notes Nell said: 'You stay right here, my lad, and we'll have this wretched thing finished before lunch! I suggest a picnic tea for this afternoon. We could take the car and explore the island a bit. What do you say, Eden?'

'Lovely idea,' and as she passed she touched Nell's shoulder gratefully. 'We'll make it a celebration now that your report is finished. Thanks for the offer of your company, David, but we'll all relax when this chore of yours is out of the way!'

David returned to his portable typewriter with good grace, and Dr Ashby barely looked up from his writing-pad as Eden went into the house.

Joel was at the gate with Turpin when Eden came out in riding breeches, and under cover of mounting her he gave her low-voiced instructions.

'They've just left for the hospital, Miss Eden, so you go in the front gate of Dayspring and take the track that runs off to the left through the trees. It curves round to the house and I'll be waiting for you somewhere along there.'

She glanced at the hospital farther along on another headland as she turned into the driveway, hoping that the prescription Dr Brandt was making up would take more than a few minutes to get ready. Joel was waiting for her near the house and he tied Turpin by the boundary wall.

'When you leave, go out that little gate, Miss Eden. You'll find a track that'll take you back to the main road. Now, that's Mr Justin's room up there, the first one after you get to the top of the stairs. I'll stay down here and I'll tell you as soon as I see the car coming back.'

Eden raced lightly up the iron stairs and on to the graceful upper veranda. Justin's long windows were open and she tapped on the woodwork and went in.

'Hallo, darling,' he said from his bed in the corner, and she gasped when she saw the drawn lines on his face. 'It's all right – I had quite a night but I'll be up in a couple of hours. I'll be back to normal then, but this has put paid to my trip and I have an idea that was what was intended!'

'The film,' she whispered, holding his hand to her cheek. 'What have you done with it?'

'It's quite safe, I promise you. I only wanted to see you so that you wouldn't worry too much, and the telephone just isn't safe on this island – that's how they must have found out I was leaving, when I made my reservations on the Trinidad plane to Washington. Stupid of me, but as I told you last night I've been a bit stupid over lots of things! I thought I could guard my horrible invention but whoever is after it is cleverer than I when it comes to desperate measures.'

'For heaven's sake put the thing in the bank vaults or send it away by registered post or give it to the police to keep for you till you're ready to hand it over!'

'Darling, have you *seen* our bank? It's only a branch office which doesn't possess a vault and which puts its faith in a couple of safes. This invention is worth world power and immense wealth in the wrong hands and I daren't leave it in the safe of a country bank. Same with the police, they're nice chaps but this is a law-abiding place and what chance would they have against the people who killed Roger and who are determined to possess this formula? As for the post, I daren't trust our honest and rather haphazard arrangements with mail on Caravel.'

Eden shivered. 'But your life's in such danger—'

'No it isn't. I'm safe as long as nobody can lay hands on the formula, because they'd be well and truly sunk if I were dead and they still hadn't found it. Please, sweetheart, stop worrying about danger to me, because it doesn't exist. What I have to do now is get off this island quickly and quietly—'

Eden glanced round as the iron stairs vibrated under hurrying footsteps, and a moment later Joel appeared.

'Car coming back,' he told them, and then left them to say good-bye alone.

'He'll keep us in touch with each other,' Justin said, and his brilliant blue eyes softened as he looked up at her. 'I'll never forget how you looked at the ball last night – you were the loveliest thing I ever saw.'

'I did my best – for you,' she whispered close to his lips, and they kissed with desperate longing before she rose to her feet and hurried after Joel.

The picnic that afternoon was a fair success. They drove a few miles along the coast with wooded slopes rising high above the road on one side, hills thick with all shades of green foliage and blazing with the red-gold of the immortelle blossom. One bay after another curved in half-moons far below the road, and near one end of the island David guided the car down to a sandy deserted beach.

He an Eden went into the water before tea, the other two preferring to relax in the shade of the trees and do nothing at all. Eden tried to look like a girl having a good time but it was an effort to respond to David's boy-out-of-school spirits and she was glad when Nell waved to them and held up the kettle. While she dressed among the shrubs at the edge of the beach she decided she ought to tell David that she knew quite definitely that she would never have more than a mild affection for him. She felt such a fraud when she gave him pleasure by seeking his company when all the time it was merely a ruse to keep him and her father quiet. He would have to be told soon, but if she did it now it would make life so appallingly difficult, and she wanted Justin to be free of all anxiety regarding his invention before he tackled her father. She sighed as she contemplated the obstacles to a pleasant future and then she went to join the others round the picnic basket.

'Thanks for helping me out this morning,' she said to Nell while they strolled along the beach later. 'I knew I was sunk if you wouldn't, so I took a chance and you played up, bless you.'

Nell frowned. 'I'm sure I don't know why I did it, but when I looked at your face the words came out before I could stop them. Eden, what's the end of all this going to be? I'm torn between two camps and I can't be loyal to everyone.'

'The end is that I'm going to marry Justin,' Eden said, glad to have matters clear between them. 'At the moment he's very involved in work but as soon as that's finished he's going to talk to Father. That's going to mean trouble as you know, and we don't want to start a family crisis before we're ready for it.'

'Crisis is an understatement,' Nell muttered. 'David's going to take it hard too, and he'll regret it for the rest of his life that he had the bright idea of us all coming to Caravel.'

'No he won't. He'll be more furious than anything else because what he feels for me is mostly possessiveness. He "discovered" the jungle waif and he assumes that finding is keeping! I wish you could have a real talk with Justin – there's so much to him that one would never find in a boy like David. He's in bed with some sort of fever but he should be all right tomorrow. That's why I was so desperate to see him this morning.'

Nell grunted. 'I can wait. I said before that he was a charmer and I hope you know what you're doing!'

Eden smiled and said nothing. She knew what she was doing, and she could wait too if she had to, but for Justin's sake she didn't want to have to wait too long. He was so alone, and he needed her even for daily companionship; they would be close friends as well as lovers. Her smile faded as she thought of his present position, and she wondered if he had thought of a way of leaving Caravel 'quickly and quietly'.

That was something she was unable to find out for several days. On the evening of the picnic Kara Brandt called at Wayfarers as she sometimes did to see that all the household arrangements were satisfactory, but this time her anxiety over Justin was obvious, and Eden knew a chill of fear. Could his condition be due to something more than he had thought?

'My father thinks it is some sort of virus,' Kara said. 'He says it has probably lain dormant in Justin's system since his last attack when he was in the army, but it is not the kind of thing we can isolate and so my father cannot be sure of the most effective treatment yet.'

'I'm so sorry,' Nell said with a swift glance at Eden's face. 'We'd be glad to help in any way possible, and both Eden and I have nursing experience. Are you looking after him by yourself?'

'So far, yes, but it may be necessary to remove him to

the hospital. His rest is very troubled but when he is awake his head aches badly and his temperature is high. But thank you for your offer of help and I will remember it if it should be needed. Now I must return because I have left his man Joel with him, and we have Mr Dinsmore and Mr Randolph coming for dinner.'

'Dinsmore!' Eden exclaimed, and Kara looked at her with raised eyebrows.

'That is so. We arranged it when we were at the ball last night. I tried to telephone them but they have gone in the yacht to Canzonet for the day and so the engagement must stand as they are coming straight here.'

Eden bit her lip as Kara continued to look at her with question in her eyes, and then after a moment Kara nodded to them all and returned to Dayspring.

'Competent chaps, those Austrians,' Dr Ashby said thoughtfully. 'I don't suppose they would welcome a second opinion from me. On the other hand, I have had a lot of experience of tropical fevers.'

Nell gave him a brisk nod. 'There's no harm in asking, Charles. Go up first thing in the morning before they leave for the hospital.'

About to beg her father to go and see Justin there and then, Eden swallowed the words and went out to the garden. He would always do his best for suffering humanity but the fact remained that he hadn't liked Justin from the beginning and it wouldn't be a good idea to make an issue of personal feelings now.

She sat reading in the garden hammock until it became too dark to see, listening hopefully for Joel's approach through the trees. But he never came, and she stayed there through the short twilight, blind to the glory of the ever-changing sky as the sun seemed to drop straight into the sea. In her mind's eye she saw Dinsmore a welcome guest in Justin's home, and with him the too-sleek cynical Paul Randolph.

After a restless night she rose at dawn and stood at her window gazing across the trees at the roof of Dayspring. Her whole being ached to be with the man she loved but she hesitated when she thought of the consequences such a wholesale burning of boats would entail.

She made a pretence of eating breakfast, simmering inside with impatience and anxiety until her father drank the last of his coffee and strolled off to call on Justin.

'Calm down,' Nell murmured as she and Eden settled on the veranda with a pile of magazines. 'I'll ask all the necessary questions when he comes back.'

'Bless you, Nell. It's such a relief to be able to talk to you about it.'

'I can't keep on being a hard-hearted Hannah when I see you looking the way you do. Sometimes it seems to me as if you're – frightened.'

'No, only anxious,' Eden said lightly, and turned her head away lest Nell should see that it was true and that she was afraid as she had never been in her life before.

When Dr Ashby returned he stood looking down at David who was sorting out a heap of Peruvian photographs.

'Did Fontaine ever take drugs?' he asked abruptly, and Eden gasped.

'Drugs?' David echoed. 'Why no, I'd say he was the last person to do anything like that. Is that how his illness seems to you?'

'Difficult to say. Brandt wasn't over-thrilled to see me, but he was puzzled over this fever too. Fontaine had all the symptoms of an overdose of drugs, but though we searched the place thoroughly we didn't find a trace of anything.'

'You searched the place?' Eden repeated, and her father shrugged.

'It was Brandt's idea and it was the sensible thing to do. After all, we wanted to know what was causing this state, and Fontaine himself couldn't tell us. His man Joel stays with him all the time, and the strongest reaction we got from Fontaine was when Brandt asked Joel to leave while his master was examined. Fontaine shouted "No!" and then started to sit up, and Joel stood there like a rock and refused to move. Odd business altogether, and I swear Joel knows more than he'll admit.'

'Is Mr Fontaine *seriously* ill?' Nell asked. 'I mean, you don't think his life's in danger, do you?'

'No,' Dr Ashby admitted, 'as long as he doesn't get any worse. If he starts recovering now he should pull through all right, but the devil of it is that we don't know the cause of his trouble. Brandt was for taking him to the hospital and running all sorts of tests, but we've decided to see how he is this evening.'

The lawn and the hibiscus bushes merged and receded in front of Eden's eyes, and with an effort she got to her feet and went indoors.

'Coming for a swim?' David called, and she half-turned.

'No – not this morning. I – I have lots of letters to write and I promised myself I would get them out of the way today. I think I'll do them in my room. It's so lovely and cool there.'

She went upstairs and after she had shut her door she stood in the middle of the room with her hands pressed to her temples. Dear heaven, what had happened to Justin since she had seen him? His head had been paining him a bit but he hadn't seemed really ill, and he was sure that he would be all right in an hour or two.

With sudden decision Eden crossed to the door, reflecting wryly that with Justin ill in bed she wouldn't be under surveillance and that for the sake of appearances it wouldn't be necessary to be under her father's eye all day. She listened for a moment at the head of the stairs and then ran down to where Beulah had just come from the kitchen quarters.

'If anyone asks, you haven't seen me,' she whispered urgently. 'How can I get out without the rest of the staff knowing?'

Beulah took her hand and led her quickly into the linen-room, across to the other side and through a door leading to a short passage. The kitchen was on their right and they could hear talk and laughter as they hurried past to the back door.

'Keep that way to the left and then you don't pass windows,' Beulah said. 'You want that I look out for you coming back?'

'I'll be away for twenty minutes anyway, but if you're around after that you can watch for me. Thanks, Beulah.'

Eden sped light-footed through the trees towards Dayspring, slowing only when the side of the house came in sight. She worked her way carefully round to the back, keeping among the tall bushes which grew in such profusion along the edge of the paved terrace where she had spent her first evening on the island. At the far end she halted in the shade of a tamarind tree and looked up at the first-floor veranda.

Justin's window was open but there was no sign of movement anywhere, and with a sinking heart Eden realized that she didn't know if Dr Brandt had left for the hospital or if Kara was sharing Joel's vigil at the bedside. Undecided, Eden stayed where she was, willing Joel to come to the window so that she could let him know she was there, but the minutes passed and Dayspring could almost have been uninhabited. Suddenly she saw movement beyond the long windows opening on

to the terrace and she made a crouching run to the parapet and watched through the open carvings of the stone-
work.

Two men stepped on to the terrace, Clyde Dinsmore
and Paul Randolph. They were both in riding clothes
and they looked as if they had just dropped in to ask for
their absent host of the previous evening. Then Kara
stood framed in the window behind them, smarter than
usual in a dark-blue dress with a wide white collar, and
to Eden's surprise she was laughing as if she hadn't a
care in the world.

'Coffee in five minutes,' Eden heard her say gaily, and
as she disappeared the two men strolled across the terrace.

Her heart thumping, Eden pressed closer to the low
parapet. She daren't retreat as they would have seen her
easily before she could regain the protection of the woods,
and if they came as far as the parapet they had only to
glance over to see her crouching below it, and then what
could she say? But they stopped strolling before they
came near her and they half-turned to look at the house.

'. . . wouldn't do us much good if we did have the run
of the place for an hour,' Dinsmore was saying. 'You can
bet that what we want isn't just lying around waiting to
be picked up. And even if Fontaine's dead to the world
upstairs he's got that man of his sitting beside him like a
black image.'

'Maybe he's just being ye olde faithful retainer,' Randolph said, 'and it's got nothing to do with guarding
anything. I must say I favour that lab in the woods—'

'Shut up,' Dinsmore broke in roughly. 'You nearly
ruined everything the last time you tried that. I've never
stood for violence and you know it, and I don't pay you
more than you're worth for you to half kill the goose
that's going to lay us a nice golden egg!'

'I couldn't avoid it,' Randolph said in a sulky undertone. 'He'd definitely arranged to go fishing and it wasn't my fault he was so keen on his blasted work that he wouldn't even go trolling for dolphin with the Hatherleys!'

Dinsmore grunted. 'At least it proved to you that he was keener on this particular job than he's ever been on anything! Well, he did me in the eye over that fruit-spray he gave to the Government when he knew I was interested in it, but he won't do me down a second time. All right, forget it. But we haven't much time because he won't be stuck in his room for ever, and if you fail me again you can go begging, for you'll be off *my* pay-roll! There's your girl-friend waiting for us so let's see some of your famous charm get to work . . .'

Her eyes close to her peephole, Eden watched the two men walk away from her, and perspiration ran down her back as she relaxed against the cool stone. Three more steps forward and they must have seen her, but Providence had merely brought them within earshot and then stayed their feet.

Kara and her guests remained in the room beyond the long windows, so Eden crawled on her hands and knees until she was well amid the taller shrubs before she stood up. From there she could still see the upper veranda but there was no sign of Joel and there was no way of attracting his attention without the risk of Kara seeing her too.

To her own dismay her eyes filled with tears and she sat down against a tree and searched for a handkerchief with shaking hands. Suddenly everything was too much to bear alone, and Justin's secret wasn't hers to share just for the sake of easing her burden. There wasn't anyone she could ask for help, and with chill foreboding she remembered the only other person who had shared the secret – his friend Roger who had died in Miami 'by accident'.

SEVEN

AFTER five minutes of deep gloom Eden pulled herself together. This was no time to act like the inexperienced innocent her father and David believed her to be.

The upper veranda was as still and empty as before, and with a last longing look at Justin's window Eden turned and hurried away through the trees. Beulah was hovering at the back door and as soon as she saw her mistress she came to meet her.

'You been gone nearly an hour! No, they haven't looked for you but they've been in and out and I sure was scared they'd find you gone! Miss Eden, you got a visitor. Rhody's got a day off from the hospital and she's supposed to be visiting me but it's you she wants to see. Got an urgent message, she says.'

Beulah led the way quietly and yet proudly towards the small sitting-room. She was enjoying the whole affair even if she didn't understand what it was all about, and Eden smiled a little. Well-brought-up girls didn't intrigue with the servants, but in her position what else could she do when it was quite literally a matter of life and death?

Rhody turned from the window as Eden went into the room and then waited until Beulah shut the door.

'You have a message for me?' Eden asked eagerly.

'Yes, Miss Eden. There's a letter from Mr Justin and I got something to tell you as well. Maybe you better read the letter first. There's – there's a lot of wickedness going on, and I don't like any of it.'

'Neither do I,' Eden said grimly, tearing open the envelope. 'I've just spent the last hour trying to attract your Joel's attention but it didn't work.'

She scanned the letter hastily and then sat down because reaction took the strength from her legs. Justin *had* had a relapse on the day she had seen him but he had known from the moment he swallowed his medicine that it had been tampered with. He had recognized the taste of the drug that was in it, and after that he had insisted on Joel being the only person to look after him so that between them they could dispose of subsequent doses of the stuff which was supposed to cure him. He didn't make a fuss at the time because it suited him to be seemingly helpless while he thought up ways and means of getting away. Escape was so difficult because he had no means of discovering the identity of his shadowy enemy.

'What have you got to tell me?' Eden asked Rhody.

'Well, Miss Eden, this being my day off I came to see Joel as usual and Miss Kara told me I'd have to visit with him in the passage upstairs because he wouldn't leave his master! When Joel saw who it was he told me to go into the room and there was Mr Justin lying grinning at me! At the hospital yesterday Dr Brandt was saying that he was real sick and how worried everyone was about him, and I was afraid of what I'd see when I got to Dayspring. Well, I was real happy to see him looking so good and then they told me they'd been waiting for me so that I could bring this letter to you and let you know that Mr Justin was what he called "foxing" everyone because it suited him that way. Does all this make good sense to you, Miss Eden?'

'Yes, he's explained it all to me in the letter. Oh, thank heaven for Joel! Can you wait while I write a quick reply to Mr Justin? You are going back to Dayspring?'

'Yes ma'am, I'm always there when I'm off duty and I don't mind telling you that I won't be sorry if I can go back there for good. I told Mr Justin I'd go back if he'd have me and I could have cried when he acted so pleased. Oh, I'm to tell you too that you can trust Beulah and that she'll carry any messages to the big house when I'm not here and Joel can't get away.'

'For heaven's sake!' Eden exclaimed as she found pen and paper. 'How long is this act going to continue?'

'That's what I said, ma'am, and Mr Justin said it wouldn't last longer than he could help but that he didn't want you to be worried and that you must have what he called a "line of communication". I – I heard him say something to Joel about a thing he didn't want to believe, and that's when I got this feeling that there was real wickedness in the whole business.'

'If it's about Dinsmore,' Eden thought, 'he'll have to believe it when I tell him what I overheard. And there's Providence if you like. If I'd been able to find Joel when I wanted to I wouldn't have heard Dinsmore and Randolph mentioning the lab incident.'

She wrote quickly, sealed the letter into an envelope, and gave it to Rhody who hesitated for a moment.

'I got to be careful when I come here?' she asked. 'You don't want your folks to know about you and Mr Justin?'

Eden sighed and ran a hand through her hair. 'Not yet, Rhody. They'll be told as soon as Mr Justin is free of this affair that's bothering him. It's just that we can't attend to everything at once.'

'And it means trouble every which way,' Rhody murmured. 'Pardon me, ma'am, but Joel and me couldn't help but see that you and Mr Justin weren't having a smooth road. I truly hope everything works out the way you want it.'

An hour before, Eden wouldn't have believed that anything at all would ever work out, but now that she knew Justin was all right the worst of her fears had vanished.

Dr Ashby went to Dayspring that evening as he had promised Dr Brandt, and it was more with curiosity than anything else that Eden waited to hear what her father would say when he returned.

'Fontaine seems better tonight,' he said, but there was puzzlement in his tone. 'He's weak, but he was well enough to make a flat refusal when Brandt mentioned taking him to hospital. An odd fever altogether, and of course as a mere visitor I can't insist on Brandt trying my methods if he doesn't care to do so. I haven't even been able to make a thorough examination because Brandt made it rather obvious that he was in charge of the case and that he hadn't asked for a second opinion. Very touchy about his professional reputation, I thought.'

'So are you, Charles,' Nell reminded him, 'so are you! Remember the time the witch doctor swore it was his charms and not your pills that halted a 'flu epidemic?'

'Hardly a comparable situation,' he said stiffly. 'Brandt is a civilized man and his ethical behaviour is a credit to our profession. Incidentally, I got at the truth of those rumours about Fontaine and his coloured ladies.'

'Go on,' Eden invited with a little smile as he glanced at her. 'It's always best to know the truth.'

'Well, one of them was particularly beautiful, and when Fontaine tired of her and gave her her marching orders she didn't take it quietly. After begging him to take her back and finding that it was no use she threw herself under his car one day when he was driving through Amberley. That would appear to have shaken him, and since then he has behaved more decently. Of course, he's a big landowner here, he's wealthy, and he's always been friendly with the Hatherleys, so he got out of the unpleasant situation without much trouble. People forget these things too easily where a man of substance is concerned. So although Fontaine has behaved very well to us and his past is not our business, he is not the type of man I would wish to have for a friend.'

'I quite agree,' Eden said with some force. 'Any man who could behave like that is beyond the pale.'

She grinned inwardly as Nell cast her a startled glance and her father nodded well-pleased by her reception of his story.

The bare bones of truth might be in the story but Eden knew that rumour was the lying jade she had always been and that it wasn't possible for anyone who really knew Justin to believe that this was the whole truth. No, she wouldn't care much for the man of this story, but he certainly wasn't Justin.

Next morning she sent Beulah to the Dayspring stables and while she waited for one of the boys to bring Turpin she looked wryly towards her father who was deep in a medical journal. It was so obvious that with Justin out of the way Dr Ashby felt it quite safe for his daughter to go riding without inquiring as to her destination. He had had quite a fright over her early dealings with Justin, but now he believed that the danger was past and he was inclined to be more relaxed about everything. The trouble was that the more unsuspicious he was now, the bigger would be the explosion when he discovered that she intended to marry Justin even if she had to go to law for permission.

Calabar Beach was deserted as it had been before, and after a two-mile gallop Eden rode back to the main road, reining in at the end of the path as a Daimler passed and then halted nearby.

'Eden my dear, how nice,' Lady Hatherley exclaimed as she opened the car window. 'Your dinner invitation for next week has been sent, but I would like to talk to you for a little while. Could we go over to the shade of the trees?'

Eden dismounted and the chauffeur opened the door of the car for her ladyship who looked delightfully cool in sage green with a wide shady hat to match. They crossed to the grove of trees where Eden tied Turpin's reins to a low branch and then turned to her companion who was frowning thoughtfully.

'Eden, what's this about Justin? He has been quite the healthiest young man I've ever known and now his house-keeper tells me on the telephone that he's in bed with some mysterious fever. I said I was coming to see him and she told me most abruptly that he was allowed no visitors on doctor's orders!'

'The doctor being her own father! H'm. I think Justin would like to see you, but of course you can hardly charge in like an army with banners after she told you—'

'Can't I?' Lady Hatherley laughed softly. 'My dear, if you tell me that a visit wouldn't harm Justin then Kara Brandt certainly couldn't stop me! And isn't it time you shared some of the worry which is giving you purple shadows under the eyes?'

Eden looked at the dainty figure beside her and then she met the kind wise glance.

'I wish I could, Lady Hatherley, but the worry isn't mine to share. It's nothing personal – I know Justin told you about us, but this is something to do with his work.'

Her voice tailed off into troubled silence as she realized that already she might have said too much.

'All right,' said her ladyship. 'This is something you mustn't talk about, but can I help in any way at all? I'm very attached to Justin, as you know, and with Government House connexions I can do lots of things which others might not be able to do.'

Eden stared at her in sudden hope.

'Can you think of a way of getting Justin to Washington or even Trinidad so that no one knows he's gone?'

'Tell me this much. Does Washington mean it could be important government business? I mean, would I be justified in metaphorically calling out the marines?'

'Yes, oh yes, I promise you it's as important as that!'

'Then we could have a government helicopter land on our lawn and take off again in five minutes. It's as simple as that!'

'But you'd have to send for it and you mustn't trust the telephone or the post. Justin made that quite clear, and that's why he's stuck where he is for the moment.'

'My dear, we have a top secret telephone with a scrambler! No one could possibly make sense of any message except at the receiving end. Of course, any message would have to be sent by my husband and although he's a perfect lamb he *is* inclined to be stuffy and wrapped in red tape. But he does give me credit for being fairly bright and I'm sure I can talk him into doing what we want.'

Impulsively, Eden kissed her cheek. 'He knows you're much more than "fairly bright"! Before we do anything further I must discuss this with Justin, but he'll tell me what arrangements to make and then I'll tell you. I think, if you don't mind, that you shouldn't go to see him after all. If you're going to help him to get away perhaps there shouldn't be an open meeting between you meanwhile.'

'It *is* desperately serious, isn't it?' Lady Hatherley asked, and then she tilted her chin. 'You're quite right. I shan't go to Dayspring today, but when this is all over I shall be there at your engagement party and we'll have a simply wonderful time. Dear, this is no time for tears!'

'I'm so relieved,' Eden said on a little gasp. 'Everything's been a bit of a nightmare and then suddenly you come along and make the solution sound quite feasible and even rather fun!'

She looked up as a drift of hot air touched her cheek, and she saw that the usually clear blue skies were streaked with mare's tails and that the movement of the palm fronds was no longer gentle.

'I'm afraid we're in for quite a storm unless it turns away from us,' her ladyship said. 'You go and make your arrangements with Justin and then come and tell me at once. If this does develop into one of our usual storms you won't be able to set foot outside the house and, as you said, we mustn't trust the local telephone. If I don't see you this evening I'll expect you tomorrow morning, and meanwhile I'll tell my husband what he might have to do. Now hurry along, dear, and I'll see you soon.'

As Turpin galloped homewards and they left the main road the air became oppressive among the trees and on the lower ground. Eden's hair was clinging to her temples in damp curls as she dismounted at Wayfarers and then sent for Beulah to take the horse back to the stables.

'Could you manage to see Joel when you're there?' she asked the girl breathlessly. 'It's terribly important and there isn't time to write a letter. Tell him that I *must* talk to Justin and between them they've got to think of a way for me to do it. Is that clear? And it's got to be today.'

'Sure thing, Miss Eden. I got lots of excuses for wanting to see Joel. I'll wait an answer and then I'll come and find you in your room. That do, ma'am?'

'Bless you, Beulah, that's fine. I'm going straight in to have a shower – I haven't felt so sticky since I came here.'

'Going to be a nasty storm, Miss Eden, and it ain't going to pass by this time. We'll have to have the shutters on for sure.'

Nell and David, busy with their morning stint on their

book, had moved from the garden into the shaded sitting-room, and Nell was leaning limply back in a chair.

'I can't write another word,' she said, and dropped the newspaper she was waving. 'Even a fan just stirs up more heat. How you could go riding in this!'

'Not a good idea,' Eden admitted, 'and I'm just going to have a cold shower. How's the book doing, David?'

'It was all right until we went limp! But I think we've passed the worst of the planning stage and now all we have to do is put the thing in beeyewtiful prose!'

'I'll spin you some prose right now,' Nell said, standing up, 'but it won't be beautiful. After you with the shower, Eden.'

The two women went upstairs together and Nell murmured: 'I gather you didn't believe the story of Justin's love affairs?'

'Well, there might have been a girl and there might have been a car accident, but I certainly don't believe the girl killed herself under Justin's wheels because he was tired of her.'

'The faith you have in that man!' Nell marvelled, and Eden looked at her in surprise.

'I'd trust him right over the edge of the world, Nell.'

'Just like the girl in Tennyson's poem. Remember?

'And o'er the hills and far away
    Beyond their utmost purple rim,
Beyond the night, across the day,
    Through all the world she followed him.'

'That's right,' Eden said blithely and went into her room and shut the door.

After she had showered and changed she sat on the edge of her bed listening for Beulah's return, but the light tap on the door was the first sound she heard and she smiled as Beulah tiptoed inside.

'Don't be too secretive,' she advised, 'or they'll all start wondering what we've got to hide! Well, did you see Joel?'

'*And* Mr Justin, ma'am! Miss Kara was out somewhere but we heard her coming back just as I was leaving. Well, far's they know she won't be going out any more today so Mr Justin'll have to meet you somewhere outside. She always sits with him after lunch till about three o'clock, so he'll slip out after that and meet you on the path through the woods between here and the big house. He said better make it half past three so you don't have to hang around.'

'Right. I'll go out by the kitchen door as I did last time, because I can't think of any possible excuse for wandering about outside on a day like this! I only hope the storm holds off until much later. Thanks, Beulah, and I'll see you downstairs about three o'clock.'

She sat with the others after lunch, trying to read while the wind force rose steadily and the landscape became blurred in a queer yellowish light, and then she gathered an armful of magazines and stood up.

'I'm going to snore in private,' she announced, 'so don't start thinking it's thunder! And I won't want any tea – I'll have something when I come down.'

'See that your shutters are properly fastened,' her father warned. 'You don't have to be told anything about tropical storms and the damage they can do.'

She promised to secure all her windows and then she went upstairs, excitement making her suddenly breathless. She put the magazines on the bed, attended to the windows, and then went out to the passage again, locking her door quietly behind her. At the foot of the stairs she halted for a second, almost sick with apprehension as she eyed the open door of the sitting-room which was fortunately too near the front of the house to give anyone inside a view of the stairway. But if anyone came out . . .

Without quite knowing how she managed it she sped through the linen-room where Beulah was waiting for her, and soon afterwards she was running through the trees towards Dayspring and Justin. She had to slow down because of the intense heat, and she was leaning breathless against a tree when she saw Justin come into view. Her vision blurred for an instant as she took in the pallor of his face and the lines engraved in his thin cheeks, and then she was racing into his arms and her greeting dissolved into a sob on his shoulder.

'Darling, darling,' she managed at last, 'you look quite terrible!' and then she looked up at the sound of his soft remembered laughter.

'*What* a thing to say to a handsome man like myself! Oh Eden, how I've wanted you! I've been trying to make plans and half the night I find myself standing at the window staring down at Wayfarers and dreaming of the time when nothing and no one can ever separate us again.'

He put a hand under her chin and as she nestled to it his eyes blazed with feeling and his lips claimed hers in a kiss that had a wild affinity with the gathering storm.

With his arm around her he drew her away from the path and into the deeper shadow of the trees.

'Now tell me your news,' he urged. 'I gather from Beulah that it was extremely important. My news is rather – awful, but it will keep for a few minutes.'

Eden told of her meeting with Lady Hatherley, and when she mentioned how much she had let slip she glanced at Justin doubtfully but he merely smiled and kissed her cheek. At the end of the story he stood silent for a moment and then he heaved a sigh of relief.

'Of course, a helicopter. I've been going round in circles trying to keep the whole invention secret and I never dreamed of the Hatherleys being able to help like this. My brain must be getting addled!'

'Darling, you've had a beastly time lately, what with being attacked and then being given this awful drug. It's not surprising you couldn't think straight. Now, what shall I tell Lady Hatherley?'

'You couldn't possibly reach Government House before this storm breaks, so you must leave it until the morning. Promise? All right. Ask her ladyship, bless her dear wise heart, to make what arrangements she can about the helicopter and on the day it arrives she can come here to "visit" me. Then she can decide I'm convalescent and must have a change, and in her own inimitable way she can sweep me off to Government House for a few days or a week-end or whatever it happens to be.'

Thunder rumbled prolonged and menacing in the distance and the trees overhead thrashed angrily in the rising wind.

'We've got a few minutes yet,' Justin said, 'and I'll see you safely back to the door. Darling, will you ask Lady Hatherley to lose no time over sending for the helicopter? I've found out who's behind the attempts to steal the formula, and they're pretty clever.'

Eden grasped his arm. 'Dinsmore? You know it was Randolph who hit you in the lab that day.'

'Dinsmore's just after anything he can get hold of, and he's only guessing that I'm on to something new. No, I'm afraid the real villians of the piece are Zeitler and Brandt and Kara.'

'Are you *sure*? But – it's unbelievable!'

'That's what I thought when the facts simply hit me in

the face and I couldn't ignore them. You see, the drug that put me under couldn't possibly have been given to me at the ball or it would have worked hours earlier than it did. But after we came home Kara made tea because her father can never go to bed without it and I usually join them. Well, the tea seemed stronger than usual but I drank it down, and sure enough I woke up a couple of hours later feeling deadly. I'm no beginner in the field of dangerous drugs and I knew someone had slipped me a Mickey Finn the previous evening, but I was in no state to work out the implications then. All I was sure of was that someone had listened-in on my call to Trinidad airport and that they'd succeeded in preventing me from getting away that morning.'

'But you didn't suspect the Brandts when I saw you that morning? Kara had just gone to collect your medicine, remember?'

'Yes, and it was the first dose of that medicine that put me on my guard! The effects of the drug don't last very long and I knew I was getting over it, but smaller amounts in a supposed cure would keep me helpless for as long as I was taking it. When I felt the same symptoms starting up again I realized the danger I was in, but I was sane enough to insist on Joel staying with me all the time and after I told him what was going on nothing would make him leave me.'

Eden gazed at him, aghast, and as she shivered he held her more closely.

'It's better to know the enemy,' he told her, 'and now I want you to keep right out of their way. Don't come near Dayspring on any pretext at all, not even if you're told I'm asking for you. I'm afraid they've guessed how I feel about you, and when people like that are desperate they have a nasty little habit of getting information by threatening harm to those one cares about.

'People like that?' Eden echoed when she heard the sombre undertones of his voice.

'They're not Austrian refugees,' he said grimly. 'It was after I discovered that they were responsible for my illness that I remembered that first dinner-party at Dayspring. The significance of what was said only struck me last night. Who but dyed-in-the-wool Nazis would say that Mendelssohn and Marx weren't typical Germans because they were Jews?'

EIGHT

EDEN walked through the trees with Justin until they came within sight of Wayfarers, listening dry-mouthed as he told her of all he had learned about the supposed Austrians. Dr Brandt was no fool and Justin had had to take small amounts of the drug so that he would still give the feverish appearance necessary to keep them unsuspicious. But he was well enough to stand in the shadows of the upper gallery at night and watch Zeitler and the Brandts in their desperate search for the formula they knew he possessed.

He realized then that when his own gas had made him unconscious in the lab that Kara had seen the notes on the bench beside him and that neither she nor her father had believed his story of an overdose of an anti-malarial drug.

'But you should have got out of Dayspring as soon as you knew about the Brandts!' Eden exclaimed. 'You'd have been safe at Government House, for example, and the Brandts and Zeitler are only three people on their own.'

Justin shook his head. 'That's just what they're not, my darling. Whoever I ran to would have been in trouble too, and how could I do that to my friends? South America and some parts of the States are crawling with ex-Nazis who managed to escape from Europe before being rounded up by the Allies, and these isolated groups aren't strangers to each other. Of course, I was completely half-witted not to think of danger in my own house, but it must have been so easy for the Brandts to watch me after I'd discovered that gas and then to take my letter to Roger out of the post-bag on the hall table. Rather than foul their own comfortable nest here they got in touch with colleagues in Florida, and poor old Roger must have been under surveillance from the minute he heard from me.'

'But you can't *know* all this, can you? And after all, Roger was killed and they got nothing for their pains.'

'It all fits, though. It was only a last-minute impulse that made him post the formula to me instead of carrying it on him, and it was by the mercy of Providence that I happened to be in the post office here on the day his envelope arrived. And what price the people who so kindly rushed him to hospital? The normal thing to do with an accident like that is to call an ambulance and the police. I'm sure Roger's pockets and briefcase were well and truly searched by those Good Samaritans!'

'Dr Brandt looks so benign,' Eden said helplessly, and then she gripped his arms while the branches tossed and thrashed above them. 'Justin, don't go back! No one could get past the sentries at Government House! Please, darling, it's sticking your head in a noose to go home now you're out of it. I'll send Beulah to tell Joel where you've gone and he can follow you later.'

'The film is hidden at Dayspring,' he reminded her, 'and I can't leave it there. I'm safe for the moment, sweetheart, and I'd rather not start anything by disappearing now. When you see her ladyship in the morning tell her about the Brandts and Zeitler, and if Sir Mungo passes it on to Washington they'll know what to do about it. I suggest they start digging at the Florida end if they can trace the people who took Roger to hospital.'

'You're a stubborn mule,' Eden despaired, 'and I can't think why I love you so much!'

'But you do, and I love you and that's all that matters!'

Large drops of rain started to fall with a harsh rustle and the thunder seemed nearer and much louder. Eden turned reluctantly away as Justin gave her a gentle push at the edge of a clearing and she started running towards the house which was almost hidden now behind a curtain of rain. Knowing that he would still be standing watching her she turned to motion him back to the shelter of Dayspring when a blinding light seared her vision and she felt she was in the centre of the most terrifying noise she had ever heard.

Deafened and with every nerve quivering she saw Justin plunging towards her and as he pushed her violently to one side her world dissolved in a nightmare of crashing boughs and a deep well of darkness.

There were moments when she seemed to float up from the dark, when she heard quiet voices and the repetition of her own name. But it was too much trouble to answer and soon she would drift back to oblivion.

Then there came a time when she didn't want to keep her eyes closed and she opened them slowly and looked around her. First of all she was conscious of a constriction about her head and her cautious exploring fingers touched a bandage. Then the shoulder of the hand she was using began to throb with a dull ache, and she frowned at a white counterpane and the brass knobs of an unfamiliar bed.

Suddenly frightened, she closed her eyes again and tried to think. Something had happened . . . she had to meet Justin . . . oh yes, the woods, and the storm making everything so dark . . . and he had told her about the Brandts not being Austrian after all . . .

The Brandts! The message for Lady Hatherley!

Effort making her heartbeats thunder in her ears she tried to sit up and then she stared blankly round the room she had never seen before. Diffused light came through the shutters and not far away the sea swished lazily on a beach.

'B–Beulah,' Eden managed in an odd little croak, and Dr Ashby and Nell hurried into the room.

'About time you deigned to notice us,' Nell said lightly. It's all right, my dear, a tree came down on you after it had been struck by lightning, but you got away with slight concussion and a bruised shoulder.'

'This – this room,' Eden faltered, looking up at her father as he counted her pulse rate and stared grimly into space. 'I don't remember it.'

Dr Ashby grunted. 'That's hardly surprising. It's a bedroom on the second floor of the Harbour House hotel in Araquilla.'

Eden gazed at him in horrified disbelief and she could feel the blood drain away from her face.

'Tell me you're joking,' she pleaded, as Nell sat on the bed and placed an affectionate arm about her.

'You mustn't look like that!' Nell exclaimed. 'I – he's not joking I'm afraid. After we found you in the woods and brought you indoors your father waited until the storm was over and then went and chartered a motor-launch. We've just brought bare necessities, and poor old David was left behind to clear up.'

'It can't be true,' Eden whispered desperately. 'I *won't* believe it. Where's Justin? Was he hurt too?'

Her father gave a short laugh. 'No worse than you were! He was hit by the tree too so we handed him over to Brandt who said he was taking him to hospital. A pretty picture you made to be sure – you and that roué lying side by side where you were struck down in judgement from on high!'

Eden leaned heavily on Nell's supporting arm while the bitterness of desolation flowed over her soul, and then she took a deep breath and looked at her father.

'May God forgive you for taking me away,' she said quietly, 'for I never shall. You should have trusted me from the beginning instead of giving in to an evil mind, and then none of the deception would have been necessary.'

Dr Ashby flushed an angry red and turned away to a medical tray on a table.

'You're hysterical,' he said shortly. 'I'll give you something to calm you down.'

'Put that hypodermic away!' Eden snapped. 'I suppose I've been under sedation all the time and that's how I knew nothing of the voyage from Caravel! Well, I promise you this – if you put me under again I shall leave you for good the moment I can stand on my feet! Nell! Are you still on his side?'

'Certainly not! I was to have stayed on with David but I came to look after you. I couldn't stop your father from bringing you here but he had to take me too. Charles, I'm warning you, leave her alone!'

'You too?' he asked bitterly, and then slapping the hypodermic on the tray he stalked out.

Eden leaned back on her pillows and gave way to the tears she wouldn't shed in front of her father. But once started it was difficult to stop, and at last she lay exhausted, pounding her fist on the bed in agony of mind.

'Come on, let me bathe your face,' Nell said in a worried undertone. 'My dear, you mustn't give way like this – we'll find some way out. It isn't the end of the world, and if you and Justin are meant to be together then nothing can stop it.'

'Only death,' Eden whispered, closing her eyes. 'Only death. That's what's breaking my heart, Nell. I was Justin's ransom from the pit and now I've left him with those devils who have such nasty little ways of finding out what they want to know. They won't waste any time either, because they must have guessed as soon as they heard he was meeting me in the woods that he had been foxing them all along.'

She looked up at Nell's concerned expression. 'You don't believe a word of it, do you? You think I'm raving! Oh Nell, I wish I was! Listen, I think I'll have to tell you everything, but promise you won't breathe a word of it.'

'All right, I promise,' Nell said doubtfully. 'But lean back, dear, because that was quite a bang you got on the top of your head. Go on, I'm listening.'

When Eden had told her everything that had happened from the time she found Justin unconscious on their first day on Caravel, Nell sat staring at the floor.

'It's all absolutely Edgar Wallace,' she muttered at last. 'Why in heaven's name didn't Justin go for help to the Hatherleys long ago?'

'Lots of reasons, chiefly because he'd hated involving me in the affair and he didn't want to involve anyone else, and besides, how could we have guessed that the

Hatherley's telephone was safer than anyone else's and that they could whistle up a helicopter just like that?'

'From what I've seen of Sir Mungo he'll have to be awfully sure you're right before he'll do even that! Anyway, couldn't Dinsmore have given him the drug and tampered with the medicine? I mean, it's not much to go on – to say the Brandts are Nazis because they say Jews can't be typical Germans. And don't forget that Justin must have been pretty light-headed while he was working all this out in his mind.'

'You're a real "devil's advocate", Nell,' Eden said wryly. 'Don't forget that he watched them turning the library inside out one night. He was sane enough to note how angry Brandt was when Kara came to tell him that my father would like to see the patient. He refused to begin with, and then Kara said something that Justin couldn't hear and Brandt agreed to let Father go up. Yes, I know, that could have been professional jealousy, but when Father was leaving after his second visit Brandt stood talking to him along the gallery and Joel slipped into the communicating bathroom to listen. Brandt was telling Father about the girl who killed herself under Justin's car, and yet some days before that he had described Father to Justin as "a rigid Puritan of the old school". Why tell such a story full of sordid detail to a rigid Puritan unless to disgust him and to keep him away in future?'

'Could be,' Nell admitted. 'Did Justin tell you how that girl really figured in his life?'

'Yes. She was what is known as a high-white and very beautiful and she was the daughter of a wealthy garage-owner in Amberley. She could have had almost any man she wanted but she wouldn't look at anyone but Justin and he never gave her the slightest encouragement. It became an obsession with her and at last Justin had to keep all the gates locked and he never went into Amberley if he could help it. Then one day he had to go, and as he was driving along the main street the girl threw herself in front of the car and – and she was killed instantly.'

'H'm. Shocking thing for him too. You'd think people would have been kind enough not to keep the story alive.'

'They were, except for that horrible Paul Randolph. He hates Justin and he's the one who's kept the story going all this time. Father should have had the sense to know the Hatherley's wouldn't be so fond of a man with a bad reputation.'

'I'll admit that your father's attitude to you and to life in general has surprised me lately. He never used to be like this.'

'Oh yes he was! But when you stayed with us at the mission you saw far less of him because he was always at the hospital or taking surgery. Anyway, I knew you were – well, fond of him, and I was careful not to disturb the "happy home" too much while you were around.'

Nell's weatherbeaten face took on a glow of pink and she went over to straighten a pile of magazines on a table.

'I'm still fond of him,' she said gruffly, 'but that doesn't mean I think he's perfect. He never was! Well, have another nap if you feel like it and I'll go and find something suitable for an invalid diet!'

'Don't be silly,' Eden muttered, sitting forward with her head resting on her hands. 'I'm trying to think of a way out of this ghastly situation and you've simply got to help me.'

Nell pointed out, reasonably enough, that there wasn't even radio-telephone communication between them and Caravel; that a telegram sent to the Wireless Station might as well be broadcast all over the island by a town-crier for all the privacy such messages received; and that there was no guarantee that a message sent via Trinidad would be sent through on the Hatherley's scrambler telephone.

'Kharama's boat!' Eden suddenly exclaimed. 'There's no moon and I'm sure he'd take me over to Caravel if I offered to pay him well. Don't look so blank! He's the Indian who sold me those lovely materials. Nell angel, find me some beef-tea or something like that and then I'll give you a letter to take down to Kharama.'

She refused to listen to Nell's expostulations about her unfitness for the journey, and after Nell had gone out with a resigned expression on her face Eden slid from the bed and stood swaying with dizziness. She clenched her teeth and took another step forward, keeping her mind on Justin and the plight he was in without her and her vital message about the helicopter. Her father's medical bag which travelled with him everywhere was on top of the old-fashioned marble wash-stand by the wall, and by the time she reached it the nausea was passing and she could focus properly on the contents of the bag.

She was looking for a tube of stimulant tablets which was usually there and which Dr Ashby had found useful on rare occasions. He didn't really approve of them, insisting that they gave a false 'lift' to the system, but right then Eden needed a 'lift' to keep her going and she didn't care if it was false or not.

After taking two of the tablets she went back to sit on the edge of the bed, picking up her handbag on the way so that she could see what money she had and also make out a cheque to Nell so that she could get some more from the bank. But there was no cheque-book, not even the leather wallet which had held quite a sum when she last saw it at Wayfarers, and with a furious gesture Eden pushed the bag away from her.

So her father had removed the last of her independence, had he? The money in her account was what her mother had left to her, and Charles Ashby had never approved of his daughter having such a sum in her own right. But he hadn't been able to do anything about it – until now. And of course he couldn't get away with this for long, but the slightest delay could be fatal to her plan to reach Caravel as soon as possible.

She looked up as Nell came in with a tray.

'Have you seen my father?' she asked. 'He's taken my cheque-book and all my spare cash, and I've simply *got* to have money to pay Kharama.'

'You shall have it,' Nell promised. 'I'll just manage to reach the bank before it closes if you write your letter now. How much shall I get out? Double the steamer fare?'

'Bless you,' Eden said fervently as she hunted in her bag for pen and notebook. 'Yes, I'll offer him that much and if he wants more he'll have to trust me to get it for him later.'

'I spoke to Charles in the corridor just now and he said he was going to call on one of the local doctors, so he won't be around to wonder where I'm going!'

Eden wrote hurriedly and after Nell had gone she drank the beef-tea and tried to eat the milk pudding and fruit which had also been on the tray. Then she washed in refreshing cold water and by the time she drew on a dressing-gown she was feeling almost normal except for a few aches and pains in her shoulder.

She stood looking round the room, remembering Nell saying that they had only brought bare necessities, and wondering what outer garments she could wear that night. Then her gaze returned to the medical bag and she frowned. Something about it was bothering her, something had impinged on her subconscious mind when she had been searching for the tablets, and impulsively she crossed to the bag again and opened it. The contents were neatly in order and then, as she moved the stethoscope to one side she heard again the crackle of paper behind the lining of the bag. There was a slit at the top just under the lock and she put her hand inside and drew out a jumble of papers, her eyes sparkling when she saw her wallet among them. Hastily she riffled through the rest of the bundle, finally separating her cheque-book from the folds of an insurance policy, and then she replaced everything and sat down to write a cheque to Nell for the amount she was borrowing.

But as she opened the book she saw a letter lying between the pages, a letter which bore signs of having been read over and over again. It was almost in four pieces at the folds, held together only at the centre of the page, but the writing was still legible and as Eden recognized her mother's free-flowing script her eyes misted until at last she could see no more. She dashed the tears away, finished the letter, and then went back to the beginning.

My darling Charles,

As you have finally refused to leave this place even for a short while I am taking Eden to Araquilla for a holiday. I admit that it is I who need this change most, although she has never seen another white child in the six years of her life, but I dare not leave her alone with you lest you try again to imprint on her young mind your own dreadful conception of right and wrong. Eight years ago I came to you from a gay, loving, theatrical family, after an upbringing which you have since called "useless and pleasure-loving", but I was yours from the moment we met and I was glad to come to this desolate place because it meant living and working with you and for

*you. You know how I have pleaded with you to put in
for a transfer or even to take the leave which is your due,
but you refuse to do either on the grounds that here we
are all safe from the evils of present-day civilization and
that we need nothing which we cannot find here.*

*Dearest Charles, no man is sufficient unto himself and
we all need the contact of our fellow-man, of fresh minds,
of all the beauty of this wonderful world. For eight years
I have existed in a vacuum, and were it not for Eden and
the love I have for you still, I think I should have died
here in the jungle long ago. I cannot say when we shall
return from Araquilla because the dread of that return
may keep us away longer than I now intend. If you love
me – and you have not said so for a very long time – you
will follow us for the rest and change you so badly need.
Araquilla as I remember it is not "a sink of iniquity" as
you usually call any town, and the three of us could have
a happy time by the sea. How I have ached for the sound
of breakers and the cry of sea-birds these last years!*

*I have written much more than I had intended to do,
but I wanted you to be quite clear about my reasons for
going away. I tried to speak of them so often but you
closed your mind and your heart.*

Au revoir, my darling.

Marguerite.

Eden was still sitting gazing at the tattered paper when
Nell tapped lightly and came in.

'What's the matter?' she asked with concern as Eden
looked up at her. 'Are you feeling worse?'

Eden shook her head and pointed to the letter, and
Nell came over to the table and looked at it.

'Marguerite,' she whispered, reading the signature.
'Where did you find this? But this is private – we
mustn't—'

'Read it,' Eden said huskily. 'You've got to read it, Nell.'

Nell turned the page over with careful fingers and as she read the lines on her face seemed to deepen and her eyes grew sad and sombre.

'You see, Nell? There never was any other reason for her going away. He lied to us all. He blackened her name and her memory rather than admit that she was running from *him* and not towards the bright lights. Oh Nell, I *hate* him!'

'No!' Nell exclaimed. 'Poor Charles, what a load of guilt he has carried all these years! Eden, try to understand – he never was very articulate but he did love Marguerite even if he didn't tell her so often enough. In his anguish at the beginning he must have believed she had stronger reasons than she gave—'

'And kept up the fiction for thirteen years?' Eden asked scornfully. 'He's a fraud and a bigot and I shall tell him so! All right, we won't agree so let's forget it for the moment. What did Kharama say?'

Nell seemed to bring her thoughts back from a great distance. 'Oh, yes, Kharama. He said he was about due for a trip to Caravel anyway so he might as well go tonight, and he'll take you for the steamer fare and no more. He'll be waiting for you at the side of the hotel gardens at seven o'clock, because it will be dark then and his boat is kept about a mile from here. I said it would be only the single journey because I didn't know what you have in mind.'

'Neither do I! But I'm sure I won't be ready to come back with him. I imagine he usually reaches Caravel, sees to whatever business he does with his brother, and then gets back here before dawn. By the way, have I anything to wear?'

'Not much, I'm afraid. I left Beulah to pack all your

nice clothes and I stuffed some shirts and a dress and your riding things in a case. You'd better take my burberry – it will be too wide but about the right length. Heavens, I must be mad to let you go on this hopeless stunt by yourself!'

Eden stood up, her eyes stormy. 'It's *not* hopeless! Joel might be doing something to help right now but he didn't know about the helicopter, and the Hatherleys might not take his word for it that the Brandts are Nazis, and anyway, what's the good of sending for a helicopter if they haven't got Justin ready to step in it when it arrives? He saved my life, you know. If he hadn't pushed me when the tree came down I'd have been under the trunk instead of being hit by a bough. Nell, what happened that night? Was Justin brought into Wayfarers too?'

'It all started when one of your shutters got loose in the wind and started banging. Your father went to ask you to see to it, got no answer when he called to you, and promptly broke in!'

'So that's how he knew I was out somewhere? Well, I guess it was lucky in a way, or Justin and I might have been out in that storm for long enough. You didn't see Joel at all? I've been wondering if he went out to look for Justin after the storm began.'

'Never a sign of him. Charles rang Dr Brandt and they brought the big car down to the gates and took Justin straight off to hospital. I wanted them to leave him with us until the storm died down but they wouldn't hear of it – just went bucketing off in all that thunder and lightning. Charles was still furious about you and Justin and when he told Brandt we were leaving as soon as the storm was over Brandt actually smiled at him and told him he was doing the wisest thing. Now I can see what he meant!'

'Yes, he knew I was a danger to him because I'd been

in touch with Justin, and now I suppose he thinks I'm well out of the way! Dear heaven, how the time is crawling – I shall have grey hairs long before seven o'clock. Where did you put my luggage?'

'In my room. I'll bring your shirt and breeches and boots later, and then I suppose I'll have to decoy Charles out of the way!'

Eden gave her a tired smile and pressed her arm gratefully. There were too many problems altogether, and without Nell she couldn't have solved the biggest one of her journey back to Caravel. The stimulant tablets had revived her physically but they had certainly given no lift, false or otherwise, to the dread that was in her heart, the dread that she would be too late to help the man she adored.

She sat down at the table again and looked at the faded writing of her mother's last letter. Now that the first shock of its discovery had passed, her anger was passing too, and she was conscious only of a deep sadness. 'Au revoir, my darling. Marguerite,' she read once more, and she ached for the young wife who had ended her letter with a hopeful 'au revoir'.

After a light tap on the door Dr Ashby came in, looking surprised to see Nell sitting on the edge of the bed, and his daughter at the table.

'Is this wise?' he asked. 'Even if you won't have a sedative you ought to be resting.'

Eden said nothing and he glanced in frowning puzzlement from her to Nell who was watching him with unusual detachment.

'I found my cheque-book,' Eden said quietly. 'You must have hidden it in quite a hurry because this was pushed in among the pages when I opened it.'

'This?' he echoed and then he saw the letter. He took

a quick step forward, his eyes glittering with anger, and then as Eden just sat looking at him he paused in mid-stride and the stiffening seemed to go out of his shoulders.

'You've read it of course,' he said with dull assurance, and the other two shot a quick look at each other. They had been braced for battle, for one of Charles Ashby's black furies, but there was no fight in the man before them, nothing but this empty misery of a suddenly old man.

'Charles dear, don't look like that,' Nell begged. 'We're the only ones who know – it's not as if you spread your original story outside the family—'

'How dare you, Nell!' Eden broke in furiously. 'Wasn't it more than enough that he should have told such a lie to you and to me? She was *my* mother, and he blackened her memory after driving her away – he's as guilty of her death as if he had pushed her car off the road with his own hands!'

'And isn't that what I've been telling myself every hour of every day for thirteen years?' Charles Ashby whispered. 'I would have followed her in death if it hadn't been for you. You would have been quite alone. And then Nell came to us and I couldn't bear to tell her that Marguerite had been running away from me when she was killed. That was something I couldn't bear to think about anyway, and in my angry bitterness I said she had been running back to her old life.'

'You didn't know what you were saying,' Nell murmured pitifully. 'You were in such torment at that time that I was truly afraid of what you might do. Your feeling of guilt was such that you built a wall of deception in your own mind and you've hidden behind it ever since.'

'Are you trying to "minister to a mind diseased", Nell?'

he asked with a wry twist to his mouth, and then he dropped to a chair opposite Eden and bent his head on his clasped hands while hot scalding tears fell on the tattered page he had read so often.

NINE

EDEN looked helplessly at her father's bowed shoulders, finding this turn of events quite unexpected. She tried to recall her former righteous anger but it was all gone, and this broken stranger was taking the place of the unapproachable dictatorial Dr Charles Ashby she had known for most of her life.

Nell was still sitting on the edge of the bed, her hands clenched on her lap. Eden could tell that she wanted to comfort the man she had loved for so long but that with rare wisdom she was leaving the outcome to the two most concerned. Love had opened Nell's eyes to the reasons for Charles Ashby's behaviour, had gifted her with understanding and almost instant forgiveness.

But Nell hadn't had nineteen years of close confinement in a jungle mission, Eden thought rebelliously. She hadn't had to endure a rigid upbringing and a constant overseeing of her work, recreation, morals, manners, and clothes. And yet – how much had she, Eden, been harmed by it all? Personal freedom had been denied her to a great extent but she hadn't really agonized over that until very recently. She had a code to live by for the rest of her life, and if it was less severe than he would have liked it was still her father who had instilled it into her. How would she feel if, for some lack of understanding on her part, Justin turned away from her? Just as her father had felt thirteen years ago, but for him death had intervened before he could retrieve any of his mistakes.

Eden rose from her chair and went round behind him. The difficult tears had ceased but his shoulders were still bowed as if they carried a weight too heavy to bear, and there seemed to be more grey in his hair than she could remember having seen before.

Almost diffidently she touched his head and he sat very still.

'I understand,' she said in a low voice. 'I'm sorry – for all of us – that things happened as they did. But you've paid, over and over again, and now it's time to leave the past where it belongs. We'll put it behind us, all three of us. I haven't been very honest myself lately, telling so many lies because I thought it was the only way out at the time. I – I'm afraid I'm not saying any of this terribly well.'

She swallowed hard as he groped upwards for her hand and then held it to his cheek with a pressure that made her wince. He had no words, but all he wanted to say was in that desperate grasp of her hand.

'I'm glad we've got straightened out,' she said shakily. 'Now it's Nell's turn. I'm going to have a bath, and I'll thank you both for the use of my room when I'm finished!'

With almost blind haste she collected her towels and toilet gear and hurried from the room. If she stayed another moment she would howl and there was quite enough supercharged emotion on the loose already. While the bath was running she sat on a stool and willed the tremor in her limbs to subside. Too much was happening all at once, and when she landed on Caravel she was going to need physical strength as well as sharp wits. She took off the bandage and touched the lump on her skull. It felt about the size of a pigeon's egg, but although it was tender it didn't seem to be broken and she certainly wasn't going to set off looking like a casualty.

When she got back to her room it was empty and she sat in front of the dressing-table and looked at her reflection in the mirror. She had washed her hair and already it was feathering pale gold in the dry atmosphere, but her eyes had lost their sparkle and were a deep still brown, faintly blue-shadowed underneath. Justin seemed so terribly far away from her, and for a few seconds she tried to picture his face and to hear his voice in her mind. But she could recall neither clearly, and her expression was lost and rather frightened as Nell tapped at the door and came in with her suitcase.

'I've brought your clothes, Eden, and honestly you don't look fit to stir out of this room.'

'I'm all right, really. I – I was thinking about Justin and I'm scared of what I'll find when I get to Caravel.'

'Your father can help there in case Justin needs a real doctor. After what you've told me I wouldn't be surprised if Zeitler and Brandt have been on the staff of concentration camps!'

'Nell! You haven't told him anything?'

'There hasn't really been time, but my dear child, you're surely not sticking to your original plan of going back to Caravel without telling him?'

Eden laughed weakly and without mirth. 'I daren't do anything else! We've sorted out this business about my mother, but that doesn't mean that Father will look any more kindly on Justin than he ever has! I simply haven't the time to explain the whole story, get him to accept my estimate of Justin, and then argue him into letting me return to the island. I'm terribly glad that Father and I have come to some sort of understanding after all these years, but it's a relationship that'll have to be worked at and tried out, and it certainly doesn't mean peace and felicity for all of us for ever and ever amen! Justin is my whole life, and without him – well, I don't care very much what happens to me. So be an angel and cover my exit tonight as we first planned. Tell Father part of the story in the morning, but not the nature of Justin's "insecticide". I shouldn't have told you about that but I had to make you believe how desperate Justin's situation was.'

'I see what you mean,' Nell said after a pause. 'All right, I'll cover for you. I'm not the woman I think I am if I can't spin Charles a good tale in the morning!'

'And the best of luck,' Eden said with the first real smile of the day. 'Could you get me a packet of sandwiches and a flask of coffee while I'm dressing? By the way, I'll see to it that the Hatherleys get a message to you here after I've arrived on Caravel, so you'd both better just sit tight and wait!'

'Promise me you'll go straight to Government House?' Nell demanded grimly. 'No heroics on your own, mind! I've been giving you credit for plenty of common sense that way, but I'll feel better if I have your promise.'

'You have it. I'm not fool enough to try anything alone, and the only reason I'm going is because Justin has been through so much already to keep his invention quiet. If I knew a single high-up in Washington I'd drop the whole thing in his lap, but by the time I found the right department and then got them to believe anything I said might be too late to help Justin. And to be quite honest, that's all I care about.'

Eden was drawing on her riding boots when Nell returned with sandwiches and coffee. She said she had ordered dinner for herself and Dr Ashby to be sent up and she had persuaded him without any difficulty to send a good night message to Eden and to postpone any further discussion until later. Meanwhile he was sitting out on the balcony of his room, more relaxed than he had been for a long time as he listened to the gentle swish of the waves in the darkness beyond. Dinner was to come up-stairs just before seven, Nell said, and as soon as she heard the waiter leave, Eden was to lock her door behind her, slip the key under Nell's door, and then go down by the service stairs to where Kharama would be waiting in the gardens.

'Thank you,' Eden whispered, giving her a quick hug, and when Nell had gone Eden put out the light and sat waiting for seven o'clock. She thought of the stimulant pills and went over to the medical bag and shook a few of them on to the palm of her hand. The night to come might be a very long one, and even if she wasn't sure about the cumulative effect of the pills it would be some-thing to know that she would be able to stay on her feet. Her bruised shoulder ached dully and her scalp felt stretched tight across the lump on her head, but it wasn't physical discomfort which was making her heart thunder in her ears and making her hands damp and shaky. If anything was to startle her in those waiting moments she knew she would probably faint from sheer tension. But even the waiter's movements were quiet as he wheeled the dinner trolley to the room down the corridor, and when his footsteps had receded once more Eden was on her way to meet Kharama.

At the side gate she hesitated and peered into the dark-ness, and after a moment a shadow seemed to detach it-self from under a tree. It was Kharama, almost as in-visible as the night itself with his dark skin and even darker clothing.

'Miss Ashby? That is good. Permit me to conduct you,

as we go to the boat by the quietest route. I believe that you are no more wishful than I that we should be seen to leave here?'

Eden agreed rather breathlessly as she tried to keep up with his swift silent pace, and it suddenly struck her that this was about the most foolhardy thing she had ever done. What, after all, did she know of this man to whom she was more or less handing over her life for the next four or five hours? He was pleasant and he was kind, but above all it was his dignity that appealed to her. He was certainly engaged in some sort of smuggling with his brother on Caravel, but she was sure it was nothing very dreadful. Silks perhaps, or even rum, or tobacco – but nothing horrid like dope. She told herself, still breathless, that she had nothing but her intuition to go on, but it didn't often let her down and anyway Kharama was her only hope of a quick return to the island.

The boat was moored in a cove some way along the coast, and without any delay Kharama helped his passenger aboard and then brought out a pile of rugs and cushions from the tiny cabin. The night was mild, and Eden said she would prefer to stay outside.

'Sleep if you are able,' Kharama said as he guided the boat out to the open sea. 'You look as if you need rest, Miss Ashby, and if this journey of yours is very important it may be some time before you will sleep again. You are warm enough?'

'I feel wonderful,' Eden said from her nest of cushions. 'I'm so relieved to be really on my way that I'd be quite happy sitting on bare boards!'

'Ah, but my wife and my two daughters refuse to set foot on my fine little boat if I do not provide what they call a few comforts! So one locker is always full of these things. Now rest, Miss Ashby, and I will waken you about an hour before we arrive so that you may have your coffee.'

Eden smiled a little at the thought of the dignified Kharama surrounded by three fussy womenfolk, and then after gazing in dreamy wonderment at the brilliance of the stars in the night sky she drifted into sleep. She felt refreshed and rested when Kharama wakened her some hours later, and together they drank hot coffee and shared their food.

'My brother lives near Amberley,' Kharama said when they had finished, 'but I can put you ashore anywhere you wish. It will have to be a solitary place of course.'

'How near can you get to Government House without putting yourself in danger?'

He thought for a few moments. 'I believe I can put you ashore just outside the boundary, but there will be danger for you after that. There are sentries and patrols in the grounds, and although it is mostly a ceremonial custom to have them there they are not likely to miss you.'

'I don't want them to miss me! The quicker I can get into Government House the better, so I'll leave it to you. You know the island better than I do, and as long as you can tell me which way to go after I land it doesn't matter about any of the patrols.'

'And I am not to bring you back?'

'No, not this time, thank you. But I'll see you before long – and maybe you can look out some special material to make me a wedding dress! I don't think it's tempting Providence to start thinking about it now!'

'I shall be happy to look for that which will make you a beautiful gown, and may I wish for you all that is good? I look forward to hearing that your way ahead is clear, that all your troubles are past.'

Eden murmured her thanks but said no more. Kharama was no fool and he had probably guessed that there was more to this secret journey than a lover's quarrel. It seemed like an age since she had last seen Caravel, and yet it was only in the early hours of that same morning that she had left it.

Because he knew the island so well, Kharama was able to put Eden ashore on a tongue of rock which formed one end of a curving bay near Government House.

'Follow this bay right round,' he told her, 'and soon you will find that you are inside the boundary. There is a wall but it does not come as far down as the beach. Now, you are ready? Then God guide you, Miss Ashby.'

He helped her on to the rocks and soon she was making her way into the woods beyond the beach. It was barely light enough for her to see where she was going, and before long she was breathless and hot and wishing she could shed Nell's burberry which had been so useful on the voyage but which hampered all her movements among the trees. She met no patrols until she reached the wall of the formal gardens, and then she heard the measured tramp of a sentry on the flagstones of the terrace beyond. Going boldly forward she mounted the few steps to the terrace and found the sentry barring her way with a fixed bayonet.

'I must see Sir Mungo or Lady Hatherley,' she said quickly. 'I have an urgent message for them, and even if they're already in bed they'll want to see me. I – I'd rather not give you my name at the moment.'

Without taking his attention from her he blew a short blast on a whistle and soon two other soldiers appeared from the direction of the house. He spoke to them in a low tone and then they placed themselves one on each side of her and escorted her to the guardhouse which seemed to be part of the domestic quarters of the building. One of them stayed with her in a small bare room while the other went away, and Eden took off her coat and tidied her shirt as well as she could. She flicked her polished boots with a silk scarf, ran a comb through her hair, and then stood waiting with outward patience under the sentry's curious glance. It was almost too much to hope that the Hatherleys had been able to do anything for Justin during her absence, but nevertheless her brown eyes were eager as she watched the door of the room.

When the door opened again it was only the other sentry who stood on the threshold and asked Eden to follow him, and after crossing a courtyard, traversing passages, and passing under arched doorways, they came at last to the great hall where the Hatherleys were waiting.

'Eden! It *is* you!' Lady Hatherley exclaimed after her husband had dismissed the sentry with a nod. 'Oh my dear, we've been so worried about you! When you didn't come by this afternoon I telephoned Wayfarers and Mr Meredith said you had gone back to Araquilla! I couldn't believe it!'

'Neither could I,' Eden said, following them into the cosy study. 'It's quite a story, but first of all, do you know anything about Justin?'

The other two exchanged a glance and Eden looked at them with fear in her eyes.

'We don't know very much,' Sir Mungo told her. 'When we couldn't get hold of you I wanted to get in touch with Justin himself, but my wife wouldn't permit it! She said it wouldn't be safe to show our interest in him at the moment. However, she gave in this evening and I rang up to ask how he was getting on. After all, everyone knows we're old friends. Miss Brandt answered and she told us that Justin had wandered out into the storm yesterday and that he'd been injured by a falling tree and was in hospital.'

'Did she tell you anything else?'

'Well, only that he wasn't likely to regain full consciousness for some time.'

'I hope that's true,' Eden said with a fervour which surprised her listeners. 'Yes, I know that sounds odd, but I'd rather he stayed unconscious for a time than that these people should be able to get what they want from him.'

She told them everything that had happened from the moment she had left Lady Hatherley the previous morning, and she told them of Justin's conviction that the Brandts and Zeitler were former Nazis.

'But he couldn't possibly be sure of that!' Sir Mungo exclaimed, pacing up and down the study. 'I could blast my career and reputation to blazes by demanding their arrest without any proof at all except Justin's say-so! I mean, their backgrounds must have been thoroughly checked before they were allowed to practise medicine in this part of the world, and they've certainly done wonders for the people here. They run that hospital like a model unit—'

'But it was Justin who built and equipped it,' Lady Hatherley broke in uncertainly. 'It shouldn't be beyond any ordinary G.P. to make a good job of running such a place. Darling, I'm afraid you'll dismiss it as woman's intuition but you must remember that I never liked either of the Brandts from the beginning. Not that that makes them German instead of Austrian!'

'It certainly doesn't,' Sir Mungo agreed with something like a snort. 'They must know that former Nazis are scooped up wherever they're found, and yet they've made no attempt to live quietly or to hide from public notice.'

'Very clever of them,' Eden said drily. 'Where do you hide something that everyone's looking for? Right under people's noses! They've built up such a background and such a good reputation that they feel quite safe here. And what a perfect place Caravel is – party-lines for every telephone, a weekly steamer, no air connexions, so law-abiding that the small police force is more of a decoration than anything else, and even Government House wouldn't be here if it wasn't for the fact that this was the best building for the purpose on any of the five islands you're responsible for!'

She ceased, breathless, and Sir Mungo looked at her in frowning thought.

'All right,' he said at last. 'I'll get in touch with Washington about the helicopter and I'll ask them to send a doctor for Justin. I'll tell them what he says about Zeitler and the Brandts and his friend Roger, and after that it's up to them. I honestly can't state from my own knowledge that they're not what they profess to be, but I promise you I'll pass on exactly what Justin told you.'

'Passing the buck,' Lady Hatherley murmured wryly after he had gone into the small office where the scrambler telephone was. 'He's a dear, but he just wouldn't dare put the Brandts under arrest without more proof or suspicion.'

'No, I can understand that,' Eden said, rubbing a hand against her temple which was aching dully. 'I don't care what happens to the Brandts as long as Justin is all right. Everything's happened so quickly. He was giving a lot of thought to the future of his invention, but he never guessed that his every movement was being watched in his own house – and *I* know the Brandts are after his formula even if no one else believes it. Once he knew how urgent it was that he should get off the island there was no opportunity to ask Sir Mungo or anyone else for help, and I only got the full story in the beginning because – well, I suppose he was a bit light-headed after being attacked, and then we met and we knew straight away – that we belonged, I mean—'

'I know,' her ladyship said softly. 'It's so wonderful

145

when it happens like that, even if you have to go through fire afterwards because of it.'

She crossed to the fireplace as the water in the electric kettle boiled, made fresh tea, and put a large tin of biscuits on the table. Eden couldn't eat anything but she drank some tea and then her cup went down with a clatter on the saucer as Sir Mungo came out of the office.

'All arranged,' he told them. 'It seems they think very highly of Justin's work, so two top scientists and a doctor are flying to the naval base on Santhya. They'll get a helicopter there and they should arrive on our front lawn tomorrow morning.'

Eden let out her breath on a deep sigh. 'Thank heaven for that. But we must do something about Justin before morning – we can, can't we?'

Sir Mungo patted her shoulder even as he glanced with half-humorous resignation at his wife.

'Eden my dear,' he said, 'for a man with concussion Justin is in the best place. When our own specialist arrives tomorrow nothing can keep him away from Justin, but until then we mustn't risk moving an injured man. And if what you say about the Brandts is true, even they can't get information from him while he's unconscious—'

'But it was Kara Brandt who told you that,' Eden broke in desperately. 'How do you know it's true? I – I wouldn't trust her as far as I could see her!'

'But what reason could she have for lying about it? I'm sorry to have to keep saying IF, but if they mean harm to Justin none of them will ever dream that you've managed to get back here and they won't know there's any need for haste. And there's another thing – the storm did quite a bit of damage here, and Justin was by no means the only casualty. I was told the staff have been run off their feet with emergency treatments at the hospital, so there can't be much time to devote to the – ah, brainwashing of one man! You're worn out after all you've been through and what you need is a good rest. Everything will go like clockwork when the helicopter gets here, and sometime during the next hours Washington will be in touch with me again about Zeitler and the Brandts. Believe me, I'll move fast when I have the authority to do so.'

Eden stared down at the carpet and the beautiful Persian design was a coloured mist before her eyes. What if the authority came too late? Sir Mungo was really quite right to wait for morning and the specialist from Washington, but he only knew the story at second-hand as she herself had told it. He didn't know the precise nature of Justin's discovery, or the lure which possession of it would hold out to former Nazis still drunk with visions of power. After all, the invention was Justin's secret and it was up to him to reveal as much or as little as he wished, and it wasn't her place to go giving details of such a horrible thing to all and sundry. Her own sense of urgency came from her love for him and it wasn't to be expected that the Hatherleys could feel it in the same measure.

'I'm not worn out in the least,' she said, straightening her shoulders. 'I slept for most of the day in Araquilla, and I slept all the way across in the boat. I couldn't possibly do with any more! I'm terribly grateful to you for getting in touch with Washington, and I'll come back here some time during the morning—'

'But you're not going anywhere now!' Lady Hatherley exclaimed. 'I've had new beds put in all the guest-rooms and I guarantee you'll sleep like a log!'

Her smile faded as Eden just shook her head.

'You're very good to me, but I can't stay. I'm going to the Nurses' Home to speak to Rhody Smith – she's Joel's fiancée and she'll be able to tell me exactly how Justin is.

147

She's on day duty this week so I'll have to wake her, but she won't mind.'

'I really can't allow this,' Sir Mungo began, and Eden stood up and put a hand on his arm.

'You can't stop me, Sir Mungo. Please don't be cross with me. I came back here to do several things, and thanks to you the most important one is done. Now I'm going to talk to Rhody, and she can tell me where Joel went after the storm was over.'

'Let her go,' Lady Hatherley advised her husband. 'You can't expect her to rest easy with only Kara Brandt's report on Justin. Nurse Smith will know more.'

She came over and kissed Eden on the cheek. 'Take care of yourself, my dear, although I know you won't run any foolish risks, believing what you do about the Austrians. If you come back before dawn one of the sentries will let you in – I'll tell them to expect you. And in case we don't see you until later in the morning we'll get a message off to your father first thing, just to let him know you're with us.'

Sir Mungo begged Eden at least to take one of his men with her, but she refused the offer, pointing out that the Nurses' Home was forbidden territory to any man and that she didn't have far to go anyway. She smiled light-heartedly at them as she went out, but they still looked troubled and uncertain, Lady Hatherley more so than her husband because she was inclined to believe the truth of Justin's suspicions about the Brandts. On her own, she would really have made a job of 'calling out the marines', but with Sir Mungo in charge there was nothing more she could do than she had already done.

Even without moonlight, the stars were so brilliant that the darkness seemed less impenetrable than it had done when Eden first came ashore. She walked on the grass verge of the road, ready to take shelter among the trees if she heard a car or motor-cycle coming in either direction. The fewer people who knew she had returned to Caravel the better. Feathery palms rustled in the night breeze on either side of her, and she heard swift scurries in the undergrowth as some small animal scented her approach and ran deeper into the woods. Brought up as she had been in the Guiana jungle she knew no fear of the night noises and in fact she scarcely heard them so preoccupied was she with thoughts of Justin.

Shaded lights proclaimed the hospital and she was glad that the entrance to the Nurses' Home was on the landward side and out of sight of anyone in the main building. There was no one in the hall, but figures moved beyond the frosted-glass doors of the dining-room, and as a coloured nurse came out Eden went along the corridor to meet her. The girl was on her way back to duty in the wards and at first she was doubtful about waking Rhody.

'Just show me her room,' Eden pleaded. 'I'll be very quiet and no one will know that it was you who let me in. I – I have a message for Rhody from Joel Armstrong.'

'You have?' The girl's smile beamed. 'Rhody sure will be pleased 'cos she's been worried to death about him. All right, ma'am, her room's just along this other passage, but don't never let on that it was me that showed you.'

She opened a door and Eden slipped silently into the room. Rhody must have been in a very light doze because she sat up in bed and asked in a frightened whisper: 'Who's that?'

Eden quickly made herself known and Rhody almost sobbed with relief. The last two days, she told Eden in a low voice, had been dreadful. On the day of the storm she had come off duty and noticed in passing that the private wing was in use, and in answer to her casual inquiry an orderly had told her that Justin Fontaine had been admitted with a head injury.

Full of concern, Rhody had tapped on the surgery door and been confronted by a furious Dr Brandt who told her to mind her own business and to keep out of the private wing. By questioning the other nurses at supper she found out that Justin's 'special' was the Austrian Sister Beck, a very unpopular member of the staff recently engaged by Dr Zeitler. There was no hope of getting any news from Sister Beck, so when the storm was over Rhody made her way to Dayspring to see what Joel could tell her. But Joel wasn't to be found although Rhody and one of the other servants searched the house for him while Kara and her father were still at the hospital. Rhody then went to Wayfarers where Beulah told her that Eden had been injured by the same tree that had hit Justin and that Dr Ashby had just left for the mainland with his daughter and Miss Macgregor.

'I was just plain lost, Miss Eden,' Rhody ended, and Eden took her hand in a comforting grasp. 'Beulah told me where you and Mr Justin had been found, and I went all through the woods and gardens in case Joel had been somewhere nearby. But I haven't heard a thing about him and I've just been waiting for a message from him or from Beulah.'

'What a to-do,' Eden muttered. 'I was hoping you could tell me more about Justin and Joel—'

'I did find out a little before I came off duty tonight. I gave the wardmaid in the private wing my new silk jumper and she kept her ears open all today – no, it's yesterday now! – anyway, it seems they're waiting now for Mr Justin to come round, and she said they seemed real anxious for him to get his wits back.'

'I'll bet they were,' Eden said grimly, remembering that both the Brandts had the same cold pale eyes. 'Rhody, it'll be dark for ages yet – could you put something on and show me the private wing? I've just had a wild idea and I'm wondering if my spoon is long enough to go and sup with the devil!'

TEN

RHODY was more than willing to leave the bed in which she had tossed restlessly ever since she lay down, and she laughed softly at Eden's explanation of the saying: 'He that would sup with the devil must hold a long spoon.'

'Which devil you got in mind, Miss Eden? I reckon you haven't told me all you know, and seems to me that Dr Brandt looked like a devil when he told me to keep out of the private wing.'

'No, he's not the devil I had in mind, and you're quite right to guess I haven't told you everything. But it's for your own sake, Rhody – I don't want you knowing something that might be dangerous for you here.'

Rhody grunted as she tiptoed to the door and glanced along the silent passage.

'Huh. With you so anxious to get Mr Justin out of here I reckon I'd be a fool to stay on much longer myself. And if my Joel don't turn up by morning I'm going to the police about it.'

Eden nodded, wondering with a quickening heartbeat what would have happened to all of them by morning.

They met no one on their way from the Home to the hospital, and Rhody led Eden through the gardens until they crouched among the shrubs alongside the private wing. There was a light behind the curtains of the office, then several dark windows, and then an end window with an even fainter light glowing inside. That, said Rhody, was Justin's room, and the door on the far side of that window led into the passage but it was always locked at night. As if to give the lie to her words the door opened from the inside and someone came out to the veranda. Both girls crouched down until their faces were pressed to the earth, and the scrape of a match made them almost stop breathing until the small light went out again.

Eden peered through the branches of the shrub in front of her but all she could see was the red tip of a cigarette as the smoker stood in the deeper shadow of the veranda roof. After a moment or two someone else came through the doorway and Eden made out the white shoes and stockings and dress of a nurse. The woman started to speak rapidly and then stopped in mid-sentence.

'Remember my rule!' came Dr Brandt's voice, and it held the snap of irritation. 'Speak English at all times! In our own tongue we are apt to say too much, but in a strange language we have to think before we speak and that is a safeguard. You were saying?'

'Yes, Doctor, I beg your pardon. I was saying that the patient is still deeply asleep. It's a pity that we made the draught so strong—'

'You are criticizing my methods, Sister? I would remind you that although you held a high position in the old days you are now under *my* orders. It was sheer misfortune that with so many people injured by the storm it has been impossible for Dr Zeitler and myself to give our attention to – to the patient. Surely it was better to make him sleep rather than to tie him to the bed? He will come round when it is time for him to do so, and there is no need for haste – now. He must understand what is wanted of him, and a clouded intelligence will be of no use to us.

I must have some rest myself, so you will not call me unless the condition of the patient makes it necessary. Is that clear? I will be in my room in the main block if you should need me.'

The glowing end of the cigarette described an arc into a flowerbed and in another moment the veranda was empty and the speakers had gone inside.

'That was Sister Beck,' Rhody breathed in Eden's ear as they crawled away through the bushes. 'What's the time now?'

'I can't see, but it wasn't quite three o'clock when we left the Home. Oh, if only I could get a horse!'

'Can you saddle up and everything by yourself? Uncle Zeke's got a livery stable some ways down the road. Come on!'

Uncle Zeke must have been fast asleep but one of the stable boys poked a startled face over the edge of the loft as the two girls entered.

'Come and help, Andy,' Rhody ordered, and after pulling on a pair of jeans the boy slid down the ladder.

'What you up to?' he demanded. 'Uncle Zeke'll sure be mad when he finds out you pinched one of his horses!'

'No he won't, because my friend here needs it in a hurry. He'll get it back in the morning and we'll pay for the hire. Come on Andy, get a move on!'

The brown mare seemed docile enough, and she was in good condition and showed no objection to having a stranger mount her like this in the middle of the night.

'I'll be back as soon as possible,' Eden told Rhody when they were out on the road again, 'and I hope I'll be bringing help. Is there anywhere you could park yourself where you can keep an eye on the private wing?'

'Remember where we hid in the bushes? Well, there's a summer-house at the other side of the lawn opposite that. I don't much like staying alone in the dark, but I guess I can manage it this time seeing it's for Mr Justin and – and Joel. If I sit in there I can see if anything starts to happen in Mr Justin's room – shadows on the windows and such-like.'

'Good lass. I'll be as quick as I can. 'Bye.'

Eden rode inland, cutting across the end of the island until she came again to the coast on the far side and a white house set amid immortelle and tamarind trees. As she galloped up the drive she could see lights in the bay down below, the lights of a yacht riding at anchor. It took about three minutes for a sleepy houseboy to open the front door and he stared at her blankly as she pushed past him and went into the hall.

'Please get Mr Dinsmore down here,' she ordered. '*Not* Mr Randolph! Tell Mr Dinsmore that a lady has urgent private business with him. Hurry!'

Seeming at last to grasp the urgency of the matter the boy scuttled upstairs and Eden paced restlessly along the thick carpet which almost hid the beautiful old tiling of the hall. There was a sound from the top of the stairs and she looked up to see Clyde Dinsmore in slippers and dressing-gown, but looking wide awake and shrewd as always.

'Miss Ashby!' he exclaimed. 'Is something wrong? Come into the library – here, sit down, you look fagged.'

Eden took a deep breath. 'This is quite literally a matter of life and death, Mr Dinsmore, so forgive me for not beating about the bush. I have so little time! I have a proposition to make to you, but first I must tell you that I know you are here because you have been told that Justin Fontaine is on to something big and you want to have it for yourself. I know too that it was Randolph who attacked Justin in his lab on the morning we arrived, and that Randolph is acting on your instructions—'

'Now wait a minute,' Dinsmore broke in, his eyes

narrowing. 'You're going a bit far even if you are under some strain or other! Supposing this tarradiddle were true, you surely don't think you could prove a word of it?'

'Oh, stop it!' Eden said on a litte gasp, and she clutched her temples as her scalp prickled with what was almost panic. 'I'm not trying to blackmail you – I desperately need your help and there's no one else I can ask. You're quite right to think that Justin is on to something big this time, but believe me it's not something even you would want to touch. You couldn't use it and you couldn't even sell it to the government because they already know that Justin has invented this – this thing and they're sending for it tomorrow. No, today!'

Dinsmore whistled softly through his teeth. 'I see. Like that, is it? Well, I'm a business man, so what's this proposition you were going to put to me?'

'Justin will be going back to his ordinary work after this, and I promise you in his name that you will be given the fruits of his next agricultural experiment – if you will help me to get him out of hospital within the next two hours.'

'Get him out? You crazy? And anyway, have you the right to promise me anything in his name?'

'I'm going to marry him and only you can make sure that he's still alive by the time the Washington people arrive. He'll back me to the hilt in anything I promise you now. But I must tell you more. Listen.'

As rapidly and as clearly as she could, but omitting the details of Justin's invention, she told Dinsmore of all that had happened since the beginning. He looked at her with frowning doubt when she mentioned what Justin suspected of the background of the Brandts and Zeitler, but his eyes began to gleam as she told of her recently overheard conversation between Dr Brandt and Sister Beck.

'Could be,' he muttered. 'Could be. Randolph got thick with that Kara female so that he could have a good excuse for being in Dayspring. He fell hard for her and he couldn't see that she blocked his every approach to Fontaine or his work or his private concerns. But I saw it, and I wondered about it, and dammit she must have known what he was after and made darn sure she and her little bunch kept it for themselves. And by the way, Randolph was not acting under my instructions when he hit Fontaine! To my way of thinking, Fontaine played me a dirty trick over that fruit-spray business because he knew one of my companies would have given a lot for it. I thought I wouldn't mind getting even with him, but I've *never* stood for rough stuff and I never will.' He grinned suddenly. 'Darn good job there's no third party listening to us! Well now, it's almost four o'clock so we'd better get a hustle on. Half an hour to get down to the *Rosca* and collect some of my less law-abiding crew, pack them into the estate car and get to the hospital. Here, here! You can't fold up on me now!'

Eden had leant her head on the arm of the chair and she was crying as if her heart would break.

'I'm sorry,' she managed after a few moments. 'This was just a wild gamble and even when I was telling you all about it I couldn't believe you would take the risk of helping Justin. I'm all right now, really I am.'

'Come on,' he said, taking her arm. 'You rustle up some coffee in the kitchen while I go and dress. I was going to give you some brandy but I don't think that's a good idea – make the coffee hot and black and strong. As for helping Fontaine, maybe I'm not entirely disinterested. I had a business partner before the war in Berlin, decent little Jew he was, and I wanted him to come to the States when things got difficult for Jews. I never heard any more until after the war and then a sister of his got in touch with me and told me he'd ended up in one of those con-centration camp hospitals where the doctors liked to use human guinea-pigs. You might say I'm not very attached to former Nazi medicos who might or might not have worked in those death camps. And if Brandt and Zeitler were ordinary doctors, why did they run from the Father-land when things got hot for the Nazis? Makes you think.'

While Eden made the coffee she took two more pills from her pocket. The effect of the ones she had taken in Araquilla had worn off almost before she left the place, but perhaps it wouldn't be wise to increase the dose even if they did seem milder than she had expected. She filled a glass with water, swallowed two pills, and then poured out two cups of coffee.

'Randolph's dead to the world,' Dinsmore said when he came into the kitchen. 'He came home from a party at the Club stewed to the eyeballs, but it's just as well. What he doesn't know he can't tell, and I think if – no, *when* we get Fontaine we'll take him aboard the *Rosca*. O.K?'

'Very much so,' Eden said with a faint smile, and her relief and gratitude were so great that she could have hugged the man she had disliked so much only a few weeks before.

They arranged that she should ride back to the hos-pital, contact Rhody, and then meet the men from the *Rosca* out on the road. Depending on what she learned from Rhody they would then decide on what to do next.

Eden stopped off at the livery stables and, glad that she had her money with her, she tipped Andy liberally and told him she would see that Uncle Zeke was paid for the hire of the mare next day. Then she hurried on to the summer-house opposite the private wing and Rhody met her at the door.

'Hardly anyone's made a move,' Rhody said. 'Beck's passed the window once or twice but if anyone else had gone in the room I'd have seen the shadow. Dr Brandt put out the office light when he went off to bed, so he'll be in the room next to Dr Zeitler in the main block. How did supper with the devil go, Miss Eden?'

'Wonderful,' Eden said, breathless with excitement. 'Better than I ever dared to hope. Come on, Rhody, I can hear the car and we don't want the reinforcements to go blundering around the place waking everyone up!'

The big estate car coasted downhill to where the girls waited at the roadside and Dinsmore got out with six members of his crew all dressed in dark slacks and jerseys.

'Turn the car,' Dinsmore ordered the driver, 'and park over there without lights, right off the road. Kelly, keep with me, the rest of you follow close. Miss Ashby, if that passage door's locked right enough then Kelly's the man to open it. Are you sure one of us couldn't get away with sneaking in the front door and then unlocking this private wing from the inside?'

'Laws, no!' Rhody exclaimed. 'There's always someone at the night desk and you'd have to pass it, and there's no knowing when a nurse or sister might pop out of one of the wards. And it's no good me going in there because they know I got no business to be there. If you all aim to keep this quiet then your only way is through the outside door beside Mr Justin's room.'

'Right,' Dinsmore said crisply. 'Lead on, ladies, and the rest of you bring that stretcher.'

Like shadows the party flitted through the grounds, and while Kelly cautiously tried the passage door the others knelt among the bushes at the corner of the building. Eden could just make out Kelly's darker outline on the veranda but he made no sound as he manipulated the lock with the skill of a safebreaker. The watchers had still heard nothing when the door was pushed open and the faint blue glow of a nightlight showed the emptiness of the short passage beyond.

'Go ahead, Pedro,' Dinsmore whispered, 'you know what to do,' and the big man beside him moved catlike to the door of Justin's room and disappeared inside. Two other men went to keep watch where a brighter light showed the junction with the main corridor of the wing, and then Dinsmore touched Eden's arm and they followed Pedro into the room.

Eden barely glanced at the chair where Sister Beck was leaning back unconscious and Pedro stood looking down at her with a pleased grin; her attention was centred on the bed where Justin lay watching her entry in dazed unbelief. She bent and kissed him quickly as two more of the crew came in with the stretcher.

'No time to explain,' she whispered, 'but you're safe now, darling. Mr Dinsmore's taking you aboard his yacht until your Washington brasshats arrive some time today. Can you stand being moved about?'

'Of course,' he said in a bit of a croak. 'I thought I was done for this time – when I recognized Beck dozing in that chair – oh sweetheart, if ever anyone had a guardian angel I've had one in you—'

Eden just smiled blissfully at him and stood aside as Dinsmore waved his other men inside and supervised the transfer from bed to stretcher. He ordered the bearers off to the car, sending Rhody with them, and then Pedro put Sister Beck on the bed, tied her wrists and ankles to the bedrail, and then prepared a very effective gag.

'Is – is she all right?' Eden asked doubtfully as she went outside with Dinsmore.

'Don't worry about her. Pedro's a real artist when it comes to this line and that's why I sent him in first. One little tap in the right place and he'll put anyone out like a light! She won't be very comfortable when she wakes up but she won't come to any harm, and we don't want any alarms raised just yet.'

Pedro came out, locking the room door and pocketing the key. He waved to the two men who were watching the main corridor, and then all the remaining members of the party stole silently through the grounds while Kelly relocked the veranda door but this time he brought the key away with him. All the seats had been removed from the estate car to make room for the stretcher and it was quite an effort to squeeze in three people along each side and two beside the driver.

'Easy as taking candy from a baby,' Kelly grumbled disgustedly as the car headed for the *Rosca*'s anchorage. 'Not even a black eye to show for it!'

Dinsmore laughed. 'I only said there *might* be the chance of a fight but I'm glad it all went off quietly. Miss Ashby and I have no proof of what we believe and we'd have been in a fine old mess if someone had yelled for the police and we'd been stopped for explanations. No, it's better this way until the proper authorities can take over the – ah, villains. I wouldn't want them to cheat the gallows.'

Eden was sitting on the floor beside the stretcher, her hand fast in Justin's. As before, the mere touch of his fingers made her blind and deaf to everything else in the world. If she had lost him . . . With boundless thanksgiving she raised his hand to her cheek and kept it there until the car drew up beside the bay. The sea was calm and the launch was large, and there was little difficulty in transferring Justin finally to the *Rosca*. The principal guest suite was ready and waiting, and soon Justin was between cool sheets on the wide comfortable bed.

'You'll do,' was Dinsmore's verdict as he stood looking

down at his new guest. 'I must say I've seen concussion victims looking a lot worse than you do!'

'I don't think I could have had much of a bang,' Justin said. 'I came round when we first reached hospital after the storm, but Brandt put me out again quick! Forgive me if I say that I can't understand why *you* should have rescued me, and why Eden should look at you with quite fatuous approval!'

Dinsmore gave him an answering grin. 'She'll tell you all about it, *and* about the bargain she made with me. That doesn't mean I'm sticking to it. It savours too much of blackmail – on my part, I mean, not on hers – and though I've been a bit of a pirate in my day I haven't got as low as blackmail yet. Yes, your Miss Ashby is quite a girl. Quite a girl.'

He went out as Rhody stuck a thermometer in Justin's mouth and placed a competent hand on his wrist. Eden crossed to the mirror and looked in comical dismay at her own reflection – tangled curls, dark shadows under her eyes, a streak of dirt on her chin, and Nell's too-large burberry open to reveal a creased silk shirt.

'Pulse is too quick, Mr Justin,' Rhody was saying, 'and I reckon you ought to rest quiet for now. Miss Eden says there's a doctor flying from Washington so he'll have a good look at you when he comes. Mr Justin – you got any idea where Joel might be?'

'Why, no, Rhody. When I came round for the second time in hospital I couldn't think where I was or what had happened. All I knew was that Sister Beck was half-asleep in a chair near the bed and so I closed my eyes in a hurry because I associated her with something not very pleasant. Then I tried to think back and after a while I got as far as remembering that tree crashing down on Eden, and myself running forward, and that was as far as I could go. When I went out to meet Eden that afternoon

Joel stayed behind in my room in case anyone came prowling around and found that there was no one there.'

Rhody's lovely coffee-coloured features hardened. 'If the Brandts have got hold of my Joel I'll kill them stone-dead! Miss Eden, they're getting us some breakfast here so I'll go along now. It'll soon be light and when you come out we'll have to think of what we're doing next.'

Eden removed her coat as Rhody went out of the room and then she turned to see Justin watching her.

'Come here,' he said softly, holding out his arms, and with a little sigh she sank on to the edge of the bed and bent to the heaven of his mouth against hers.

'I haven't any words,' he said at last. 'My sweet, my love, my darling, apart from the fact that we love each other you're the finest most loyal *friend* anyone could have. Now tell me what's been happening and why Dinsmore of all people should have laid on such a full-scale rescue party. Oh – that tree didn't hit you after all, did it? All I can remember is giving you a push to one side!'

So, lying on the silken coverlet, riding boots and all, Eden told him what he wanted to know, and she felt the sharp intake of his breath against her cheek when she told how she had wakened in Araquilla after the storm and realized that he had been handed over to Brandt the previous night.

'What you've been through!' he marvelled. 'How did you possibly manage to keep going until now?'

'I stole some of Father's stimulant pills,' she said, leaning up on her elbow and smiling down at him. 'I do feel wide awake but I don't really think they're much good. Now I must get back to the Hatherleys before your brass-hats land on the lawn there!'

'Your eyes are beautiful,' he murmured, 'but they're far too bright. Darling, can't you send a message to

Government House? I don't want to let you out of my sight.'

'But the worst is over! Without you or your formula the Brandts are sunk and they may even know it by now. Sir Mungo said Washington were setting up a high-powered probe into their antecedents and that they'd be in touch as soon as possible. Once he gets the authority, Sir Mungo can send the police to gather them in, and then I can bring the doctor and the two scientist bods to you. We don't want to shout aloud that you're here until we know that nothing more can go wrong, and anyway Dinsmore said that if I insisted on going ashore he would send his tough little Kelly with me!'

He raised an arm and drew her close to him again. 'I still don't like it. I know what you have in mind – you and Rhody want to do something about Joel!'

'Rhody's been simply wonderful, and all the time she's been worried to death about him. I promise you we'll get Sir Mungo to organize a search party and that we won't go doing anything foolish ourselves. Now you simply must rest, darling. You're much livelier than I expected but you're not out of the wood yet and you'll need your wits when your brasshats arrive.'

'I'll need them the next time I meet your father! I have no intention of waiting any longer for you, and in fact I'll see about a special licence today. You *do* want that as much as I do?'

'I'd marry you this minute if I could,' she said against his lips. 'Once Father knows everything I think he'll give in, and we've got Nell on our side and she's not without influence.'

She drew away from him reluctantly and picked up her coat. 'I love you so,' she said with a smile, and she hurried away before the temptation to stay became too much for her.

Kelly was hovering nearby and he came forward to meet her.

'All right, Miss?' he asked, grinning widely. 'The gentleman didn't look too bad at all, and he'll do fine here till he's on his feet again. You'll be ready for a bit of breakfast now?'

'Not really,' Eden said as he ushered her into the dining-cabin where Rhody was sitting at a table, 'but I suppose I'd better eat something. Coffee is about all I can manage.'

'Ah now, wait till you see the lovely fruit we've got, and I'll see to your toast myself. That'll give you five minutes to have a quick wash – through that other door, Miss.'

'Sure is a beautiful ship,' Rhody said after Kelly had gone out. 'Even the soap in that cloakroom smells like heaven!'

'I'd love a bath,' Eden said, towelling vigorously after a refreshing wash. 'We daren't wait though, and once I got into warm scented water I'd probably fall asleep for a week! Rhody, we'll never be able to thank you enough for all your help, and as soon as we can we'll go and do something about Joel.'

'It was my pleasure to help, Miss Eden, and there wasn't much we could do about Joel during the night anyway. I've looked everywhere he might be, and now the police'll have to find him. You reckon the Austrians are going to get arrested?'

Kelly came in with coffee, toast, chilled fruit juice, and a large platter of avocados, bananas, oranges, grapefruit, and pineapple.

'No bacon and egg?' he asked wistfully. 'I'm a dab hand at that but no one ever wants a decent breakfast in this part of the world.'

'Sorry,' Eden laughed. 'I couldn't face it this morning but I'll take you up on the offer some day.'

She drank three cups of coffee, managed one piece of toast, and put a banana in her pocket. Rhody was sitting considering the implications of what Eden had just told her about the so-called Austrians, and after a moment she nodded.

'It fits in, Miss Eden. I loved nursing and I kept on feeling sorry because I couldn't settle down there. I wasn't happy, and I had more fear than – well, than respect for the two doctors. Hard as nails they were, and so was Sister Beck, and I thought maybe doctors and nurses had to get like that because too much sympathy with sick people might take your mind off your work. But I knew I couldn't be like them and I thought I just wasn't suited to nursing.'

Dinsmore came in and poured himself a cup of coffee.

'Kelly isn't a cook or a steward,' he said drily, 'but since I told him he was to look after you two he seems to have taken the order literally! I would have sworn he was the toughest member of the crew, so it just shows you.'

'I liked him,' Eden said with a smile. 'It's very good of you to let him come with us.'

'I'd come myself only I'd rather stay aboard while Fontaine is here – just in case we have to start repelling boarders! Now then, straight to Government House and no detours. Wait for whatever message Hatherley gets from Washington about the Austrians before you go tearing around looking for this Joel Armstrong. And if it sounds as if I'm laying down the law it's because I wouldn't trust the Brandts an inch until I knew they were locked up. If they're part of a group with contacts in Florida, nobody knews how many groups there are or even where they are.'

'I agree with you,' Eden said soberly. 'All right, Rhody, let's go. See you later, Mr Dinsmore, and – anything I say by way of thanks is quite inadequate, but you know how grateful I am for everything.'

'So help me, I enjoyed it. It's a long time since I had the chance of leading a raiding party!'

Dawn had flared up shortly before and the sea glittered in the morning sunshine as the launch made for the jetty where the car still waited. Kelly quickly replaced all the seats and as he and the two girls drove off, one of the crew went up to Randolph's house. That gentleman would still be dead to the world, but Dinsmore wanted the houseboy warned not to say anything about Miss Ashby's visit in the middle of the night. The less outsiders knew the better.

Kelly waited in the car while Eden and Rhody went into Government House, and Eden was surprised to see Lady Hatherley up and dressed at that hour.

'Thank heaven!' her ladyship exclaimed when she saw them. 'I've been imagining the most frightful things all night and I hardly closed an eye. Did you find out how Justin was?'

'He'll be all right,' Eden said non-committally. 'This is Rhody Smith, and we're both very anxious about her fiancé who's been missing since the storm. You know – Justin's man Joel Armstrong.'

'Why, of course! Oh, we must do something about that at once.'

She hurried into the office to come out in a few moments with her husband who looked as if he hadn't slept much either.

'I've been staring at the telephone,' he said ruefully, 'willing the wretched thing to ring. You gave my conscience a bad night, Eden, making me wonder if I'd done the right thing. Now, what's this about Joel?'

He listened to Eden's story and then nodded.

'Last seen in Justin's room at Dayspring? Right, I'll ask the District Super to send a police detail out there. It will also give us a chance to find out who's there and who's at the hospital – just in case your hunch about the Austrians was right, Eden!'

He went out to telephone the Superintendent of Police, and Lady Hatherley gripped Eden's arm.

'The more I think about it the more sure I am that your "hunch" was right! If we've left Justin in the hospital – just because of a little red tape – if the helicopter or the message from Washington are too late to help him—'

'Stop worrying,' Eden soothed her. 'Justin is far away from the hospital and perfectly safe. A – a friend and I really stuck our necks out last night and we kidnapped Justin and put him aboard the *Rosca*. But let's not say any more about it until we hear from the F.B.I. or whoever are digging around in the Austrians' past. I don't mind for myself, but I roped in an awful lot of people to help me last night, and if there are any cans to carry back *I'll* do it!'

Her ladyship dried her eyes with a dainty handkerchief. 'Justin's a very lucky man and I think he knows it. Bless you, my dear, you've got a great heart.'

The colour rose in Eden's cheeks as she turned away to the window. She didn't feel that she had done anything requiring great courage. She had had to improvise every time she met an obstacle, never sure that she was doing the right thing, not daring to be hopeful of success. What would have taken greater courage than she felt she possessed would be to go on living if she lost Justin.

Rhody dozed uneasily in an armchair, Kelly read a paperback in the driving seat of the car, and Eden and

Lady Hatherley went to join Sir Mungo in staring at the telephone. There was one message on the local line from the sergeant in charge of the police detail at Dayspring. They had searched the house from attic to cellars without finding Joel or anyone but the household staff. Kara Brandt's bed hadn't been slept in, and neither she nor her father were to be seen.

'So they must all have spent the night at the hospital,' Eden said thoughtfully. 'Zeitler always sleeps there, we know Brandt was there, so probably Kara joined them when they decided they were about to get what they wanted from Justin. They'd finish him off afterwards of course, and it would be all nice and legal with an unimpeachable death certificate and a slap-up funeral to follow.'

'You *can't* believe all this,' Sir Mungo muttered, and perspiration stood out on his brow. 'They'd never have got away with it—'

'Of course they would,' Eden said scornfully, 'if we hadn't taken Justin away last night. They don't dream that I know as much as I do about Justin's invention, and they probably wouldn't get away with it in the end. But by then Justin would have been dead, and what good—'

She turned away, biting her lip as she heard her own voice rise in shrill protest. Her endurance was wearing thin and she knew she wouldn't be able to stand much more. Then she spun round as a bell rang in the office and Sir Mungo hurried to the telephone.

'You were right,' he told Eden jerkily as he came out with a revolver and holster in his hand. 'I've just been on to the Super and he's meeting me at the hospital with all the men he has. The F.B.I. scooped up a nest of former Nazis in Florida by connecting them with the death of Justin's friend Roger and working from there. They want our little lot taken in and they don't seem to mind how we do it!'

'It's a pity they're in the hospital,' Lady Hatherley said with anxiety. 'Still, you may be able to take them by surprise. Do be careful, darling, and remember that this is a police job and not yours.'

Eden doubted very much that the doctors or their womenfolk would give any resistance. If they had already found Sister Beck bound and gagged on Justin's bed they must know that their particular game was up. Nazis in a tight spot had a habit of taking poison and there wasn't much that this bunch didn't know about drugs and their uses.

'Could we go to Dayspring now?' Rhody asked. 'Maybe the police have found some sign of Joel outside, and they said none of the Brandts was there when they rang up.'

'Yes, it should be safe enough now,' Eden said. 'Rhody! When you were looking for Joel did you go near the lab?'

'Why – why no, Miss Eden! I didn't go that far. You think maybe he's there?'

'Well, if no one's looked there yet I guess it's just possible, but don't bank on it, Rhody! We'll find the police in the grounds and we'll tell them about it.'

Lady Hatherley, her mind on her husband's possible danger, waved to them rather absently as they ran out to the car. Kelly was glad to hear that the Nazis had been cornered, and with a sympathetic glance at Rhody's set face he started the engine. As the police would be somewhere in the extensive grounds of the estate he drove the car to the end of the track outside Wayfarers and then turned it.

As Eden got out she could see the roof and part of the top storey through the trees and it seemed such an age since she had last been inside. With a small sense of shock she realized that David must still be there, and that this was the first time she had thought about him since she came ashore. Poor old David, he certainly hadn't made much impression on her mind or heart.

'Up that way, I think,' Kelly said, pointing along the path. 'When we get to the top we're bound to spot a cop somewhere. Hey – Miss Ashby – you all right?'

Turning too quickly to go up the path Eden saw the trees waver in a fantastic dance and she swayed as she put out a hand to grasp something. Rhody steadied her and then looked at her anxiously.

'You can't keep going no longer, Miss Eden. Mr Kelly, you wait here with her while I run and find the police-men—'

'No,' Eden said, opening her eyes cautiously. 'I'm all right now. It was just a sudden dizzy spell. Kelly, you go with Rhody and I'll go into the house here and wait for you. David's still here and I don't suppose he's heard much of what's been going on.'

'I'd forgotten all about Mr David,' Rhody said dubiously. 'All right, Miss Eden, you just go in and sit down till we come and collect you.'

They went with her as far as the front door and then she told them to go and see about Joel and they both ran back down the path and away through the trees. Eden stood in the familiar hall, listening to the chink of crockery from the kitchen quarters and hearing David whistling his favourite air from 'the Mikado'. She entered the sitting-room just as he came in from the terrace on the far side, and he stood and stared at her in open-mouthed surprise.

'You – you're in Araquilla,' he muttered. 'There's been no steamer – you can't have come back—'

Eden giggled weakly. 'Oh, what a tale have I to tell! D'you realize that Brandt and Zeitler are a bunch of Nazi death-camp doctors? Imagine finding a nest of v-v-vipers on this paradise isle!' She giggled again. 'Ooh, you keep on disappearing! David, be a lamb and get me a glass of water – what a shtate to be in on thish happy happy morn—'

She collapsed into a chair by the door and David hurried forward.

'Water,' he repeated. 'Yes, you sit still and don't worry about a thing. I'll look after you.'

Eden fished around in her breeches pocket for her last two pills, barely noticing when David dumped a glass of water on the small table he pushed up beside her before he hurried away again.

'Kill or cure,' she said hazily, and swallowed the pills with the water. Then she leaned back until her surroundings stopped their crazy gyrations, only opening her eyes when she heard footsteps on the terrace again.

'Here she is, sir,' David was saying. 'Obviously it was that bang on the head, although I can't understand how she got back here. There's no sign of her father or of Miss Macgregor, but in her present state I wouldn't put it past her to have swum from the mainland!'

Eden's mouth opened but no sound came out. Behind David stood Dr Brandt and he no longer looked benign. His white hair was awry, his eyes burned with fury, and the hand in his pocket gripped what was obviously a revolver.

ELEVEN

'So it *was* you!' Dr Brandt said in a low tense voice. 'When we found Beck bound and silenced I knew that you had had a hand in it somewhere—'

'Wait a minute!' David interrupted, his face a study in bewilderment. 'What's all this about? I brought you here because Eden seemed to have gone off her rocker—'

'Be quiet, fool!' Brandt snapped, and David went white as the doctor brought out the revolver and prodded him with it. 'This woman has ruined everything for us but now we can use her – no one will use force to try to stop us while we have her as a shield.'

'Dear heaven,' David whispered, 'what have I done?'

He whirled on his captor, but without apparent effort Brandt clubbed him with the butt of the revolver and David went reeling through the terrace doors and collapsed outside.

'I do not wish to rouse the patrols with a shot,' Brandt said grimly, 'but I will risk it with you, Miss Ashby. Do not think that I will leave you here alive so that you may enjoy the future with your lover! Get up.'

'I – can't. I only came in here to rest because I was feeling ill – all right, stop waving that gun at me – I'm coming—'

Desperately playing for time she tried to remember how long Kelly had been gone. Surely it was time he came back for her—

'I have little patience left,' Brandt said viciously. 'Were it not that I am also waiting for my daughter you would be dead by now! Move!'

Eden gripped the back of the overstuffed couch and walked slowly towards the terrace windows which Brandt was indicating when she heard the crunch of footsteps on the front path.

'Kelly!' she screamed, and dropped to the floor behind the couch. 'He's got a gun!'

A bullet thudded into the upholstery and while she waited in terror for Brandt to look over the top and fire point-blank there was a tattoo of pounding footsteps through the doorway.

Kelly's language was really choice, Eden thought hysterically as she tried to get to her feet, and when she looked over the top of the couch he was twisting Brandt's arm behind his back until the revolver dropped from his nerveless fingers.

'Eden – Miss Eden,' Kelly was calling desperately, and she managed to croak at him.

'I'm – not damaged,' she said with a gasp. 'Just scared out of my wits!'

'And it's no wonder! I can hold this old buzzard as long as you like but when you feel up to it you'll find a whistle in my pocket. If you blow it at the front door the police up in the woods'll hear it – we got the Armstrong lad, by the way, tied up but not hurt.'

Before Eden could summon the strength to stand properly upright someone else came running along the terrace and Kara halted inside the room with horror in her gaze.

'Father,' she whispered, and Eden scuttled forward on all fours to pick up the revolver from the carpet. She more or less scooped it on to her lap because panic had drained the strength from her fingers and she couldn't have held a pin.

'You have the money?' Brandt asked, his face agonized as Kelly took a firmer grip on his arm. 'Then, go! The others are already waiting. It is a command!'

Kara's face crumpled and she clutched a black brief-case more tightly. 'We will not leave you! I will fetch the others—'

'It is too late!' Brandt rasped. 'You have a start of five minutes, no more! I say that you will go – you have never disobeyed me – this is my last command!'

With a sob Kara turned and ran through the terrace doors, and Kelly swore with deep feeling.

'I'm sorry,' Eden said. 'I just couldn't hold that gun, and I'm still not sure if I can walk. She won't get far – they'll have found out by now that there's no one at the hospital.'

Kelly edged towards her with his prisoner and she put the gun in his disengaged hand.

'I'm not afraid to use it either, ye old devil,' he told Brandt grimly, slightly relaxing the grip on his wrist. 'Got the whistle, Miss Eden? That's right, take it easy.'

Eden got to the front door, gathered her breath and blew the whistle as hard as she could. It didn't sound very loud to her but there was an answering hail from the woods and several policemen came into view. She raised her hand and they started to run, and then she weaved back to the sitting-room having just remembered David lying unconscious on the terrace. But there was no one there and she blinked uncertainly in the brilliant sunlight just as the engine of a motor-boat shattered the quiet of the bay. She turned round as the policemen came in, in time to see Kelly relax his grip of Brandt completely, and the doctor's other hand flash to his mouth. The poison was quick but it wasn't pretty, and Eden sank to a chair and leaned her head down on her knees.

Kelly came over and touched her shoulder and she straightened slowly. Her surroundings still had a distressing tendency to float about, but she was wide awake and her brain was clear.

'He waited till the last minute,' she murmured. 'When he heard the boat he knew Kara and the others had got away, and when the police came he knew he was really finished. Kelly – have a look outside, will you? Brandt hit David with the gun and he went spinning out there somewhere.

Kelly asked one of the policemen to go and then he drew his finger across the black hole in the centre cushion of the couch.

'That's a bullet hole,' he said, and his horny finger shook slightly. 'I hope you'll never get nearer the next world than this before your proper time! We'd just caught up with the police in the wood when I thought to myself, dammit who *is* this David you and Rhody were on about, and I legged it right back here to keep an eye on you like I promised. I heard you yell just as I got to the front door, and Brandt was so mad at you that I was on to him before he could turn on me. How the devil did he happen to be here instead of at the hospital?'

'Goodness knows – unless they found Beck before it was light and got away without anyone seeing them leave. Somehow they dodged the police who came to hunt for Joel, and they must have got round David because he was still thinking they were the cat's whiskers when he brought Brandt to attend to me! Poor old David, I think it was the biggest shock of his life when he found out what he'd done. I hope he's all right and that they haven't taken him aboard the motor-boat instead of me. Kelly – be a dear and go to the baize door at the other end of the hall. The servants have probably got their heads under the kitchen table, so please calm them down and send the one called Beulah to me. I might as well change into something decent while I'm here.'

'Now, Miss Eden you can't take much more. You look just fine and you should sit right here till you're fit to come out to the car and go back to Government House.'

'I'm sick of the sight of myself,' Eden said firmly. 'I can't stand this shirt for another minute and I don't intend to. I'm walking on cotton wool, I feel as light as air, but I have all my wits and I'm hanging on to them. Go get Beulah.'

With a resigned expression Kelly did as he was told, and with many exclamations Beulah rushed in and then helped her mistress upstairs. A stinging cold shower helped to make Eden almost human again, and she dressed in the clean underwear and the green silk dress which Beulah had laid out..There was the sound of much coming and going downstairs and when Eden strolled back to the sitting-room Sir Mungo was looking at the bullet hole in the couch.

'All over,' she said with a sudden spurt of laughter. 'No one got hit and that's the main thing. Oh – David—'

David was having first aid from one of the policemen and he flushed as he looked up at her.

'I wasn't properly knocked out,' he muttered. 'When I stood up I saw that the sailor had Brandt under control and that you were all right, so I raced off to the Dayspring beach. The motor-boat was supposed to be Kara's birthday present from her father and he came early this morning to invite me to spend the day with them. I see now that they just wanted the cover of Wayfarers until they were ready to leave – but it was all so normal, and Brandt was making fun of Kara because she insisted on going back to the house for something she'd forgotten.'

'Their money,' Eden said, 'and it wasn't a case of forgetting it! They had to wait until the police were out of the way before Kara dared to go for the briefcase. They were excellent actors, and of course they had to be, with the life they lived. You were lucky, David. When you'd served their purpose they'd have put you out of the way.'

'Yes, I know that now. Anyway, while we were waiting for Kara I decided to come back for my camera and that's when you walked in. Well, if you'd seen and heard yourself! You scared me silly and all I could think of was getting a doctor for you as soon as possible!'

'He hasn't told you the rest of it,' Sir Mungo said. 'When he went racing off from here he went along the cliff top behind Zeitler and the Beck woman, got down to the boat which was drawn up by the trees, and did for the steering because he had no time to mess up the engine. As it was he just managed to slip away among the trees when Kara Brandt and the other two ran along and got the boat into the water and under way. They got out of the bay all right – but with the steering gone they went with the current eastwards. We saw it all from the headland. The Brandt girl jumped into the water when she saw what was happening but she didn't have a chance because they were right on the edge of the whirlpool—'

'The Cockpit!' Eden said, and she shivered, remembering that sinister patch of deeper blue water which claimed its victims with such effortless ease. 'How horrible! But – one way or another it's all over. I think – shall we get back now and wait for the Washington people?'

Kelly's ready hand was under her elbow and they went out to the estate car where Rhody was sitting with Joel's hand clasped tight in hers. Eden touched his shoulder and they smiled at each other with quiet content.

'Could I trouble you to drop us off at Dayspring, Mr Kelly?' Rhody asked. 'Joel's had cramp real bad after being tied up since the storm, but I'll look after him now. Miss Eden, maybe you'll tell Mr Justin I'm back in my old job? He said he'd like to have me back when I could, so it's just as well to start off now. Tell him me and Joel will look after everything till he comes home again.'

Eden promised to pass on the message, wondering with a catch of the heart if she too would be 'coming home' with Justin.

Back at Government House she sat in a trance of contentment while Sir Mungo told everything to his wife and to the three officials who had just arrived by helicopter. She knew she was on the way to Justin, and the exclamations and congratulations didn't make much impression at all.

'People have been decorated for less than you have done,' said the senior scientist, looking down at her with an approving smile. 'You'll probably end up with a letter from the President himself!'

'Nice of him,' Eden murmured vaguely. 'All I want is my father brought from Araquilla and his consent to my marrying Justin. Are we ready to go now?'

She didn't miss any of the indulgent looks exchanged by everyone present. They thought she was light-headed, almost at the end of her tether. But she felt fine. Just fine.

Kelly looked after her jealously all the way back to the *Rosca* and he didn't leave her until he had handed her over to Dinsmore who was looking almost gleeful at the head of the accommodation ladder.

'Welcome aboard!' he greeted her. 'That man of yours has just about gone mad since you left!'

Eden introduced him to the new arrivals and then they all trooped down to the guest suite where Justin was watching the door with his intent blue gaze.

'Hallo, darling,' Eden said brightly. 'We've arrived—'

She certainly had. Without any warning a blanket of darkness descended on her and she fell into deep comfortable oblivion.

She wakened slowly to a feeling of well-being and as she stretched luxuriously she heard the strumming of a banjo in the distance.

'When you've quite finished wallowing in silken sloth,'

someone murmured, and Eden turned her head to see Nell sitting sewing beside her.

'Nell! How did you get here? Is it steamer day?'

Nell laughed and bent to kiss her lightly. 'Nothing so common! I thought you said you had no friends in the Government hierarchy? A plane was sent from Santhya to Araquilla to pick up your father and me, we got V.I.P. treatment when we landed there, and then we were brought here by helicopter. The tales we heard about Eden Ashby would make even your hair curl, and Charles could hardly believe it was his daughter they were all talking about!'

'How silly,' Eden said impatiently. 'If anyone dares to call me a heroine or anything stupid like that I'll – I'll hit them! My motives were completely selfish. I wanted Justin and I made sure I got him. He's getting on all right, isn't he? And why isn't it dark yet?'

'Because you went to sleep the day before yesterday and because the time is now early afternoon! Charles and I have already been here for two nights, and I must admit that staying aboard this yacht is my idea of bliss!'

'Yes, the yacht,' Eden murmured. 'Were you very surprised to find us here?'

'In the beginning, yes, but not after we'd heard the full story. Clyde Dinsmore certainly came up trumps when you went to him for help. By the way, Kharama brought me a parcel for you on the morning after he got back and he said to tell you that no matter how far he looked he would never find anything more suitable for your purpose. And when I saw the material I knew why you wanted it!'

'My wedding dress,' Eden said excitedly, pushing back the sheets. 'Oh Nell, where's the parcel – I can't believe I've been asleep for so long – oh, do you think Father will give his consent without too much argument?'

179

Nell laughed. 'Calm down! You needed that sleep after the pills you'd been taking and the energy you'd spent. It seems you passed out in front of the doctor who had come from Washington so you got the best of attention on the spot! Justin told him about the pills so he gave you a good going-over and then they sent for Beulah and popped you in here to sleep it off. As for your father's consent, he was rather subdued when he found out how much you were prepared to risk for Justin, and he was what you might call in a receptive mood when he met Justin here. Actually, they've been getting on very well, and when I last saw them they were lolling in the shade on deck with Clyde and having a lazy argument about politics. Yes, it's "Clyde" and "Justin" now, but of course Charles gets "sir"! David was invited to join the party but he preferred to stay on at Wayfarers, and although he has accepted the situation I don't think he particularly wanted to be around while you and Justin planned your future. Beulah is making your dress because we knew there wouldn't be much time to spare once you woke up, and Kelly is playing the banjo and waiting to be told that Madame is awake and wants to be fed. And Madame's private bathroom is through that door over there!'

'Golly,' Eden said, awed, as she looked at the appointments of the bathroom. 'This is a floating palace all right. If you'd like to give Kelly a shout you can tell him I'm ravenous and that he can let himself go on the ham and eggs this time. I want to be clothed and fed and in my right mind before I see Father or Justin!'

Beulah had brought some of her clothes from Wayfarers, and when she was ready Eden chose a slender sheath dress of yellow wild silk with sandals of the same shade. She brushed her hair until the feathery curls gleamed golden, and then she went out to the sitting-room of the suite where Kelly was putting the final flourishes to an appetizing meal.

'That rest did you a world of good, Miss,' he said admiringly. 'Now, if you want more coffee or another helping of anything just you ring that bell.'

By the look of the table Eden doubted that she would want any second helpings for a week, and even with a little assistance from Nell there was more than Kelly approved of to clear away at the end of the meal.

'I feel a new woman,' Eden said, going back to the night-cabin to wash her hands and to take a last critical look at herself in the mirror. 'Nell, what's Kharama's material like?'

'Like a heavy organza and it's shot here and there with gold thread but not too much of it – the loveliest stuff I've ever seen. Of course Beulah and I left the choice of sleeves and neckline and things like that to you, but there was quite a lot Beulah could do and she's just getting on with it. This white thing I've been making is one of the underskirts. If you like we could get Beulah to bring the stuff in now.'

'No, let's leave it. I – I think I'd better see Father first. Don't leave us alone – it will be easier if you come back here with him.'

'Nervous? You needn't be, I promise you, but I'll stay if you'd rather.'

When she came back with Dr Ashby, Nell strolled into the night-cabin where she was just out of earshot, and after a long look at his daughter the doctor went to her and kissed her gently.

'You seem quite recovered,' he said, 'and very happy. What hurts me still is that you had to go through so much alone. If only you had explained more in the beginning, or even in Araquilla—'

'Would you have listened?' Eden asked quietly. 'And if you had listened, would you have believed me?'

He drew her to sit beside him on the divan and he kept her hand in his and looked down at it.

'No,' he said after a time. 'Perhaps I would neither have listened nor believed. I've been wrong about so many, many things. Forgive me, my dear. You know, the hospital is now without medical staff, and a doctor from Santhya is acting as locum for the time being. Justin has asked me if I would like to take over, and if I agree, to choose my own assistants.'

'Oh, how wonderful! You will, won't you? You've been far too long in the jungle and you've already left a splendid memorial there in the hospital you built. And I'll be at Dayspring – at least – you *do* approve of my marrying Justin now, don't you?'

His grasp on her hand tightened. 'There is no one I would rather give you to than to Justin. He's a very fine man, as I would have found out sooner if I hadn't been so prejudiced! So you would like me to come to Caravel too? It appeals to me very much. Do you think Nell – I mean, she has such an interesting career – dare I ask her if she would stay too?'

'*Please* ask her! I'm not going to do your courting for you, so you just ask and find out for yourself!'

'All right,' Charles Ashby said with a little breathless laugh. 'And now I suppose I'd better tell Justin he can come in. He's pacing up and down the deck at the moment. Eden – he's about all you want in this world, isn't he?'

'Yes, he is,' she said quietly. 'That doesn't mean that I want to shut everyone else out, but what I feel for him is something apart and quite wonderful.'

'Then remember to tell him so now and again. I don't think he could care more for you than he does, and I don't think he'll forget to show it. That was where all my mistakes began – I didn't speak of my love. Never be ashamed to let your love be seen – wear it with pride—'

He kissed her quickly and went out, and Eden hardly saw Nell follow him because her eyes were misted with tears. Her father had learned through anguish and bitterness that love had to be nurtured and cherished to be kept alive, and he wanted no such sorrow to touch her and Justin.

She got to her feet as the door opened once more and then she was in Justin's arms and the old enchantment was turning her blood to fire as his lips found hers.

'I love you,' she said after a breathless interlude. 'We have all the time in the world for explanations but right now that's all I have to tell you. Just that I love you.'

'That'll do to be going on with,' he said huskily, and he lifted her into his arms and sat down still holding her. 'My small golden angel, my love, my darling, marry me soon?'

'Yes, oh yes,' she whispered, and her fingers trembled in ecstasy against his dark hair as he bent to her mouth again.

'This is how it should have been from the beginning,' he said, cradling her to him. 'No fear of being seen by someone who wouldn't approve, no rushed meetings, no narrow escapes from injury or worse because I'd involved you in danger when I had no excuse for it. You should have been wooed and won in peaceful surroundings—'

'I was won that very first morning,' Eden said contentedly, 'but I'm not at all averse to being wooed now. Carry on.'

The fingers of his free hand moved through her hair and she caught her breath as she met the intensity of his gaze.

'That's going to take the rest of my life,' he said, 'and

perhaps it's not a bad thing after all that we should start with our wedding day. Can you be ready the day after tomorrow? I've got the licence and everything's arranged. The Hatherley's are holding the reception at Government House, and Clyde will go to Dayspring for a week if we would like to honeymoon on the *Rosca*. Does that idea appeal? We can go anywhere you like, of course, but the privacy of this yacht for a short cruise is worth considering.'

Eden glanced round the cabin and her eyes sparkled.

'She's a beautiful ship and I think it's a heavenly idea! How kind everyone is being to us. Poor Lady Hatherley, she was in such a state because Sir Mungo couldn't see the urgency of getting you away from Brandt.'

'You can't blame him, darling. A governor isn't all-powerful, you know, and it would have been very sticky for him if he had acted on his own and then found that your theories were mistaken after all. *We* both knew they weren't mistaken, but it was quite a tall tale for an outsider to swallow.'

'What about your formula?'

'I didn't have to go to Washington myself when I saw who they'd sent here, so although the Defence Department have the formula they can't do much with it while they haven't got the antidote. I shall continue to work on that, but not to the exclusion of my usual experiments, so they can't let the stuff loose on the world quite yet! I believe I'm well on the way to finding the antidote, but as I say, I'm not rushing it!'

'Where had you hidden the film, by the way?'

'It was so simple it was funny! I took the piece of film out of your locket on the night of the ball and I picked up a briar pipe which had got broken weeks before and which had been lying on the mantelpiece ever since. I'd bound the stem with sticking plaster but I'd never used it, and it must have been quite a familiar sight to Kara. So I wrapped the tiny pieces of film in oilskin from a tobacco pouch, stripped the plaster off the pipe and then replaced it with the film underneath it. And there it stayed until I handed it over the other day! We'll never know if the Brandts knew they were searching for a tiny piece of film like that, because as far as I know the only thing they had really seen was the page of notes on the day Kara found me overcome by the gas. It's odd – they'd still be comfortably ensconced here if they hadn't been tempted by the dream of the power my horrible invention would have given them.'

Eden smoothed his cheek with loving fingers and he turned his head to press his lips against her palm.

'Justin darling, I hope you'll never make another accidental discovery like this last one. You'll have to invent a preparation that will make figs grow on thistles, just to rid us of the memory of gas warfare.'

'And give the invention to Clyde?' he asked with a soft laugh. 'Oh yes, I'm sticking to the terms of your bargain with him because I want to do it, but he intends to back out. I think we'll get round the old buccaneer by telling him he can pay a small royalty for whatever I hand over to him!'

'That's that settled,' Eden said happily, 'and I think Father has quite made up his mind to take over the hospital here, and he'll be so grateful for Nell and she'll be in the seventh heaven because she's loved him for years.'

'And she and Lady Hatherley will run the island between them and have a whale of a time! As for David – he's still very young and he'll go off to Mexico with the rest of the expedition and some day he'll find the girl who was really meant for him. Now then, is there anything else you want to know about anybody, because I want to talk about us.'

'Nothing else,' Eden said as he shifted cushions on the divan and settled more comfortably with his arms about her. 'Do let's talk about us.'

'Who wants words?' he murmured, and speech and laughter were stilled as they turned to each other and were lost in a world of their own.